Desert Shadows

DESERT SHADOWS

Marion Wentzien

AVALON BOOKS
THOMAS BOUREGY AND COMPANY, INC.
401 LAFAYETTE STREET
NEW YORK, NEW YORK 10003

PRINTED IN THE UNITED STATES OF AMERICA
BY HADDON CRAFTSMEN, SCRANTON, PENNSYLVANIA

To Louise A. Vernon,
teacher, mentor, friend

CHAPTER ONE

"You are not going to panic, Judith Nelson," I said aloud. Ahead of me the road dipped out of sight. Everywhere I looked there were cactus, scrub brush, and dirt. There hadn't been a car or truck in what seemed like hours. I couldn't remember when I'd last seen a building with inhabitants. I glanced at the gas gauge, which showed half-full. On the temperature gauge the needle hovered unpleasantly near the red zone.

"There's no doubt about it," I admitted five minutes later. "I am definitely lost. Lost in the middle of nowhere." It would be dark soon. The car was sounding more and more like a broken washing machine on its last cycle. I realized that in my anxiety I'd stepped harder on the gas pedal, as if I could magically zoom myself to safety.

Do what you tell your physical-therapy patients to do when they're feeling overwhelmed, I counseled myself. *Take a deep breath. Hold it. Let it out.* I inhaled the hot, dusty Arizona air and let my breath out slowly.

As soon as my breathing became normal, I forced myself to think back. Where had I gone wrong? There'd been that spot, right after I'd turned off the highway. I'd had a choice. It had seemed logical to turn right onto the better road. But maybe I should have turned left.

"Come on, Matilda," I said, calling my yellow compact car what my younger brother Hugo had named her. As I made a U-turn, I tapped the steering wheel. "Don't let me down. We're buddies, remember?"

Ahead of me the ragged mountains glowed a velvet purple. Behind them the late-afternoon sun sent red streaks into the brilliant-blue sky. Off on the right, crumbled adobe walls testified to some ancient dwelling that had been reclaimed by the desert. Behind me the black road rolled away—completely empty, not a car in sight.

"Uncle Jeremiah likes solitude," Mom had said. For some reason I hadn't understood what she meant. Now I did. The hairs on the back of my neck prickled. I longed for the clang of buses, even taxis honking. In this desolate countryside you could scream for a year and nobody would hear you. Of course, they said that about big cities too—that you could be mugged, scream for help, and nobody would come.

But in Chicago I'd never felt like that. I'd taken comfort in the bustle of humanity. If *I* screamed, somebody would help me. I'd believed that even as a little girl. Of course, maybe I'd figured that if nobody came I could help myself, I thought wryly. Being the only girl in the middle of four brothers had taught me self-sufficiency if nothing else.

I'd reached the spot where the road forked. Slowing to a crawl, I scanned the ground for a broken sign—anything to give a clue.

"You take a right off the highway," Mom had said. That hadn't been a problem; I'd done that. "About three quarters of a mile along you'll see the old sign to the ranch. At least, I think it will still be there. But knowing Jeremiah. . . ." Her voice had trailed off, the way it always did when she talked about her maverick uncle. Impatient to get on my way, I hadn't pressed. If only I had. . . .

Oh, well, no point in thinking of that now. I swung the steering wheel and headed Matilda toward the foothills. The sky was a blaze of reds, pinks, and eye-hurting oranges. Deep-violet shadows stained the desert.

The flatness of the desert ended abruptly, caught by rolling foothills dotted with scrub brush. As the foothills grew steeper, I noticed huge barren areas on them. It looked as if a bulldozer had come through, stripping the land. Cacti lay strewn like soldiers on a battlefield. Such wanton destruction; I could hardly bear to look.

There was a barbed-wire fence on my right. Behind it five square-faced Herefords stared back at me. A fence. If there was a fence, there must be civilization nearby. I took another deep breath. Then I saw it. The rusty old sign. BBs or buckshot had pocked the letters almost beyond recognition.

Silver Sands Guest Ranch. 4 miles. Behind it, propped up against a cactus, was another sign. In the fading light it was hard to read. Finally I made out, FOR SALE—*ranch, cottages, outbuildings, water, 2,800 acres.*

"The ranch will close at the end of May for the year. Jeremiah's written that he has three interested buyers," Mom had said in her campaign to get me out here. "By the time you get there, the ranch should be sold. You'll have two weeks to get him on his feet, literally and figuratively. He can be a stubborn old goat, and without Anna to push him, heaven knows. . . ." She'd shaken her head.

The main reason her uncle was selling the ranch was that his wife of forty years had died four years ago, and I knew Mom was feeling sad that she hadn't seen more of the two of them. She'd spent most of her childhood vacations on the ranch. Then she'd married Dad and had us kids, and time had gotten away from her. "So be prepared," she'd said. "I just hope he'll come back here with you."

I jerked my mind back to the present. The arrow was in the red zone now, but I was afraid if I stopped to let the engine cool down, I'd never get the car started again.

Once the sun set, it was as if a shade had been drawn. It was simply night without any preliminaries. I switched on the headlights. Suddenly a jackrabbit skittered into the road and stopped, mesmerized by the lights. I slammed on the brakes. Matilda sputtered and jerked to a halt. The rabbit streaked safely into the brush.

I wiped at my face with the back of my hand, waited a second and then turned the key in the ignition. The engine purred into life. There was a pop, a sizzle, and hot steam began pouring out from under the hood.

I sat for an hour and a half. *No one's going to come,* I warned myself finally. *If you don't take some action, you'll have to spend the night here.* That idea wasn't appealing. An almost-full moon was sliding up into the sky. I'd gone at least another mile after the sign. So it could be only about three miles to the ranch. At home three miles wouldn't be much for me to jog. On the road, with the light of the moon to guide me, I should be all right.

I got out of the car. It was very quiet. Not giving myself time to think or feel, I pulled my suitcase out of the trunk and exchanged my sandals for tennis shoes. On impulse I grabbed a sweater. Then I stuck the suitcase back and slammed the trunk shut. Was there anything else I should take? Maybe the half-finished, now very warm can of soda pop from a pit stop along the way. Just in case I got stranded and needed a drink. It would be better than nothing. I locked Matilda, took one more deep breath, and started out at a slow jog.

Off in the distance there was a wobbly howl. Then another. A giant shiver slid from my neck down the length of my spine and into my heels. If there'd been a full moon, I would have looked around for were-wolves. The howling could only come from coyotes, I decided after another few tense moments. Mom had told me about falling asleep listening to them as a child. She'd found them comforting. I found them scary. I picked up my pace. Three miles. At home I could do a twelve-minute mile. But the road was rough. I didn't want to fall.

Somewhere in the distance a low roar sounded. It was a sound I knew I'd heard before but for some reason couldn't identify. The road dipped down into a gully and then up again. The noise was getting closer. It sounded like thousands of angry bees. I slowed my stride.

Suddenly over the hill ahead of me a light appeared. Then a lot of lights and not all confined to the road; some were lurching over the desert. *Motorcycles*. That's what the noise was. I pressed my hand to my lips, scared. I scrambled off the road to keep from being mowed down.

I heard a surprised "Hey!" and knew I hadn't been fast enough—that I'd been spotted.

Blindly, tripping, ripping my pants, catching my shirt on the brush, I ran into the desert, trying to get away from them. A root or something tripped me, knocking me down with a bone-aching thump. The can of pop flew from my hand.

I looked up at the thick wheel that seemed to be only feet from my body. *He's going to run over me,* I thought, frantic. But the machine stopped inches away, sending up thick, choking dust. Before I could get to my feet, the beam of a flashlight held me captive. Behind the glare I could make out the snapping black eyes and white teeth of a man who was straddling a huge three-wheeled all-terrain vehicle. He motioned abruptly, and all the engines shut off. In the sudden silence the desperateness of my situation seemed more overwhelming than it had with all the noise.

"What in the world are you doing?" he asked. The other riders had stopped in a rough circle on all sides of me. There was no way I could get around them. With their faces caught by the strange angles of light and craggy shadows, they were a frightening bunch. Some wore their hair long; a couple had bandannas around their necks or foreheads. A few were on ATVs; some were on dirt bikes.

"I'm going to my uncle's ranch," I answered, thinking with a strange detachment that I sounded incredibly like Little Red Riding Hood announcing that she was going to her grandmother's house.

"You're Jerry's niece?" The wolf got off his machine and moved closer. The flashlight in his hand shone in my eyes, blinding me. "Yep," he answered. "That's who you are, all right."

I put my hand up, shielding my vision. "Do you mind?"

"Sorry." He snapped the light off. Even so, I was caught in the glare of all the headlights that seemed to be coming from a dozen different angles. He held out his hand. Instinctively I put my hand out, and he caught it in his large one, pulling me effortlessly to my feet. "I'm Rudy Valesquez," he said. "And you're Judy from Chicago, right?"

"Judith," I corrected. Removing my hand from his, I brushed at the knees of my pants. Something that felt like hysterical laughter kept threatening to bubble up and out. I was safe. He knew who I was. He knew my uncle. The edge of fear dissolved into a strange, trembling relief.

"I was up at the ranch today. He was wondering when you were coming in. Say. . . ." Rudy snapped on the flashlight and scanned the surrounding desert, as if I should have been traveling on an ATV like he was.

He swung the beam over to the road. "Where's your car?"

"It broke down about a mile or so down the road."

"You were going to walk to Jerry's?" There was another flash of white teeth.

"Somehow I knew a bus wouldn't be coming along."

Rudy laughed. Several of the other men did too. One fired his engine back into life and throttled it impatiently. "Let's not stand here all night talking," he shouted over the roar. "I've got a thirst—"

"You guys go on without me," Rudy interrupted. "I'll take Judy back to her car and see if I can get it started. If not, I'll take her back to Jerry's."

Even the blackness seemed to vibrate. Clouds of dust rose, clogging my eyes and nose, covering me with a fine film. The men's shouts, their voices lingered long after they'd disappeared from sight.

Rudy swung his leg over his ATV. "Hop on."

I moved toward him and stopped, baffled. "Where?"

"Behind me." He scooched forward and patted the wide seat behind him.

Hesitantly and not very gracefully, I swung my leg over.

The machine surged to life. "Hold on," Rudy shouted over the roar.

I put my hands tentatively on both sides of his waist, aware of the feel of his shirt, of the obvious muscles just under the thin cloth.

"You've got to hold tighter than that." Rudy reached around and took my hands, pulling my arms around him until my cheek was pressed against his broad back. "There, that's better."

Before I could react, he took off, the ATV bucking unsteadily beneath us. I held on for dear life. The wind tore at my exposed cheek. My long, straight hair turned into tiny whips, and I had to close my eyes to protect them. The heat from Rudy's back warmed the side of my face pressed against him. We seemed to be the only two people on the face of the earth, spinning through some wild territory. Night riders. It was exhilarating and scary and wonderful, all at the same time.

Within a few minutes Matilda appeared. A couple of the other bikers had stopped; the hood was up. "A water hose burst," one yelled as we approached.

"Nothing we can do about that tonight," Rudy said to me. "I can fix it tomorrow."

"Thanks. I'd appreciate it."

Rudy circled around, giving me my first ATV lesson—you couldn't back up, although he amended that, saying that some of the four-wheeled all-terrain cars could—and soon we were headed back in the direction of the ranch.

I felt a mild trepidation at leaving Matilda in the hands of the two who were still peering into her. A vision of her, gutted, popped into my mind. I thought about asking Rudy for reassurance and then caught myself. These weren't the streets of Chicago or New York, where an unattended car could be demolished in five minutes. Besides, Rudy knew the guys.

It was too hard to speak. I tried once or twice, but the wind tore the words from my mouth and scattered them across the desert. This time Rudy stayed on the road. My pants rode up, leaving my legs bare. Bits of gravel sprayed painfully against them.

Just when I thought I couldn't stand it any longer, we turned off the gravel and onto a dirt road. After another few minutes I saw with surprise that the desert had given way to a kind of civilization. Lights from small adobe cottages sparkled, giving the black night a friendliness it hadn't had before.

Rudy stopped before a large adobe building. "This is the main lodge," he told me.

"It's beautiful." After the harshness of the desert, the lodge seemed like an oasis. Large, well built, serene. From the various hanging lanterns I could see it was a whitewashed white or light pink, with thick, dark wooden beams. Through an open window came an operatic aria. The voice was rich, vibrant, with an intensity that could only come from a live performer. Mom had told me Uncle Jeremiah played host to some very famous people. My imagination took fire. I could hardly wait to see who was gifted with that incredible voice. . . .

"Since his fall, Jerry's taken to staying here," Rudy explained. "His place leaks—that's how he got injured, you know. He was patching the roof, and the ladder he was on collapsed. He fell ten feet."

"We didn't know all the details. Ten feet? A seventy-year-old man—he's lucky to have broken only an ankle."

"He's got spirit, all right. Like you," Rudy added with a chuckle.

"So that's how you could tell we were related," I teased. "All spirited people passing through these parts must be related to Jeremiah Sloane."

"You've also got the same light-colored eyes...
and the same determined chin. Even sprawled on the
ground there, you had it stuck out a mile, just the way
Jerry does when he's stubborn."

This time I laughed. How funny that a complete
stranger should peg my fatal flaw so easily. Stubborn-
ness. Mom, my brothers...they all said it was my
driving force.

"If you have any questions while you're here, just
ask me. With Jerry's bum leg, I've been helping out
—like a caretaker, I guess you could say. So I know
everything that's going on. If there's anything Jerry
doesn't need, it's to be bothered with every little detail
of running the place. He needs to get his strength
back."

"That makes sense," I agreed. "If I have questions,
I'll ask you first." I took the hand Rudy offered and
got down. My legs felt shaky.

Rudy clapped a friendly hand on my shoulder. "I'm
glad you've come, Judy. Jerry needs cheering up real
bad. And he needs someone to light a firecracker
under him—to get him making plans. I have the feeling you're just the right person for the job."

Before we could make it up to the porch, the massive front door swung open. A man stood there, both
hands propped against the doorjamb, peering out. The
singing, I realized, had stopped. Once again the night
was silent, eerie.

The man was very tall. The lights on either side of
the door seemed to bounce off his roughly cut hair,
catching bits of coppery red like tiny flames. He wore
wire-rimmed glasses that didn't hide the deep anger in

his eyes. His mouth was a tight line. He looked from Rudy to me and back to Rudy.

"Hi, Donovan," Rudy said pleasantly. "This is Jerry's niece. Judy, this is Donovan McGuire."

Donovan nodded at me and then focused back on Rudy. "Haven't you caused enough trouble for one day?" Donovan's voice was low, heavy with anger.

"My feelings about you exactly. A suggestion—why don't you stop standing in the way of progress? Let me buy the ranch."

"Never."

"Jeremiah's willing."

"Not as willing as you'd like to think."

They'd squared off, chins jutting forward, hands clenched into fists, and I was trapped between them and their angry words.

I didn't know whether to be scared or amused. They looked ridiculous. But there was an underlying deep-seated anger that felt a touch dangerous. "My car broke down," I heard myself saying, totally changing the subject—an old family ploy for tense situations. "Rudy was kind enough to give me a lift here."

My words drew Donovan's gaze like a magnet. Instead of lightening up, of saying, "How lucky for you," his scowl deepened. "Just what we need around here," he said softly. "Another helpless person."

Now it was I who felt a surge of annoyance. Helpless? I might be a lot of things, but helpless I wasn't. "Excuse me," I said, equally coldly. "But I'd like to see my uncle."

The way he was standing blocked the doorway. There was no way around him. Would he really not let us pass him? I don't know whether I would have walked smack into Donovan or not. But when I was within a foot of him, one arm dropped to his side and he turned his body sideways.

I caught a pleasant whiff of woodsmoke as I passed him, and my quick glance picked up the high arch of his cheekbones, the deep-set eyes. There wasn't a spare ounce of flesh on him. In a way he reminded me of my brother Spike. "She's here," he called out. But the words didn't have a welcome ring to them; they sounded like a warning.

CHAPTER TWO

I moved like a sleepwalker toward the huge stone fireplace that dominated the room, dimly aware of the pressure of Rudy's hand on my shoulder, as if he were steering me to a very specific destination. I could hear the dull thud of his boots on the tile floor and the echo of another's—Donovan's, I guessed. The events of the day had finally caught up with me. I felt overwrought, exhausted, and the beginning of a headache threatened behind my eyes. Although I knew there were a number of people standing, sitting, staring, I didn't look at any of them long enough to form impressions.

I stopped when I came to a plaid couch directly in front of the fire. There, propped up by pillows, was a man who could only be Uncle Jeremiah. His most outstanding feature was a puff of white hair that encircled his head like a spring dandelion. Beneath the hair was a gaunt, but once strong, face. He had a beaked nose and—yes, just as Rudy had said—light

15

gray eyes that were enough like mine to cause a jolt of recognition.

"Hello, Uncle Jeremiah. I'm Judith."

"Judith." Uncle Jeremiah held out thin, blue-veined hands and clasped my outstretched hand between them. "How glad I am to finally see you! You look just like Virginia did at your age, except you're taller." His voice was as whispery as cobwebs, his breathing labored. "She and I got the short genes. She was. . . ." His voice faded away. For a moment I thought maybe the exertion of talking was too much for him, but then I realized that he had been overcome by a memory. "Such a scrappy little girl. She rode the range like an Indian."

"Her daughter's just as scrappy." Rudy moved forward to stand beside me. "I found her hiking through the desert."

"My car broke down," I said.

"Oh, no. Not more bad luck." The color seemed to drain from Uncle Jeremiah's face. He struggled, as if to sit up. Rudy and Donovan nearly collided in their effort to restrain him.

"Uncle Jeremiah, please . . . just rest." His breathing really had me concerned. Mom told me he suffered from asthma and mild emphysema. Then I realized that the surgery on his ankle—the anesthesia used—had probably aggravated his conditions.

"Just a burst water hose, Jerry," Rudy said. "No need to get alarmed. I'll fix it tomorrow."

"I can fix a water hose," Donovan said. "Why don't you just take care of your own business? As far away from here as possible," he added through clenched teeth.

"Gentlemen, gentlemen," a melodic, rich voice interrupted. From the shadows near the fireplace a black woman materialized. *Helena Knight,* I realized, stunned. As she approached us, her high forehead drew tight in a frown, and she pressed a slim finger against her full red lips. "Don't upset Jeremiah."

Her words were much more effective than mine had been. Rudy shrugged and stepped back. Donovan, still glowering, shifted his gaze away from Rudy.

"Judith, I'm Helena Knight."

"I know. I recognized you."

She smiled, obviously delighted.

"I'm pleased to meet you," I said. *Astounded* was more like it. Helena Knight was world famous. Up close she was far more beautiful than the photographs I'd seen of her in magazines. Her hair was very short, accentuating her oval face and allowing her large brown eyes to dominate her face. Interlocking gold hoops tumbled from her nicely shaped ears to the shoulders of the sapphire-blue caftan. Her feet were bare, the toenails painted bright red.

"Jeremiah, you should be resting. Why don't I introduce Judith to the other guests?" Helena tucked her arm through mine. "We're a special bunch, you know. All old-timers or children of old-timers. Jeremiah invited us to be his last guests before he sells the place." She sighed, then threw her shoulders back and continued with her performance. "Margot, come here, dear."

A tall, angular woman detached herself from a low-slung leather chair. Donovan stepped aside to let her edge in. Margot had intense, wounded brown eyes that glanced at me quickly before she lowered her thick lashes. A sudden rush of feeling seemed to emanate from her. *She doesn't like me,* I thought, startled. *Why?*

Her very thinness made her seem as brittle as a desert wind. Her hand as it clasped mine was dry, firm—a strong hand. It was hard to determine her age, but I guessed she was in her mid-twenties. She was dressed in faded jeans and a pale yellow shirt. There were green snakeskin boots on her long, narrow feet.

"Then Susie and Chuck are our honeymooners." The two of them were sitting together on a loveseat. Susie, who was young and very blond, turned a bright red. Chuck grinned at her then at me. "Chuck's parents are long-time guests. They couldn't get away, so they sent the bride and groom. The lovely woman in the straight-back chair is Mrs. Bentley."

The white-haired woman nodded to me. "I knew your mother when she was here as a youngster," she said.

Then I met Dr. Morgansting, who had a stack of books under his arm. He was in his sixties. Mr. and Mrs. Jamison were there with their son and daughter-in-law.

"I'll never remember all these names," I said, feeling a touch of panic, the way I did sometimes at work when I first glanced at the weekly roster and saw all the new patients. Eventually I learned how to link their names with their injuries so that I could remember them.

"Don't worry. We'll keep reminding you," Mrs. Bentley said.

"How long are you staying?" Donovan asked, and I sensed Margot perk up at his question.

"I'm not sure. I guess it depends."

"Depends on what?"

"A number of things," I hedged, not sure how much family business I should unload in front of the guests.

"Donovan, since I'm incapacitated, will you show her around?"

"Don't worry, Uncle Jeremiah. I can show myself around. It's you I came to see. I'll be happy just sitting, talking to you."

"Nonsense. I won't hear of it." A flash of color rose in his pale cheeks.

"I'll be glad to show Judith the ranch," Donovan said smoothly.

"I will too," Rudy said.

I smiled gratefully at Rudy. How could I have thought he looked scary? Here in the warm glow of the fire he looked like a large rumpled teddy bear.

"I can't believe she'd have any interest in having you do that," Donovan said. "She doesn't look like the biker type."

"She took to it pretty well tonight. For all you know, she may not be in to mesquite fires and rabbit food."

Once again the two men were glaring at each other. A log popped in the fire, shattering the tension like a gunshot.

"Helena," Uncle Jeremiah said, "will you sing?"

"Certainly."

"Judith, sit here beside me." Uncle Jeremiah moved closer to the back of the couch and patted the narrow empty space. There was barely room for me to sit, but I managed. Rudy sank down to the floor near me, crossing his legs Indian style.

Helena moved away from the fire and took a seat at the piano nestled in the far corner of the room. The blackness of the baby grand gleamed. A red-and-blue-striped serape was slung cheerfully across the closed frame. Margot trailed after her, choosing a chair in a dark corner.

Helena began playing Brahms's Lullaby, singing the German words in a low voice, thick as honey. It was so movingly beautiful, tears sprang to my eyes. As I tried to blink them away, my gaze caught Donovan. He, too, was enraptured. His face had softened. He was very, very handsome, I realized with a shock. Before, his arrogance had edged his features with a sharpness. Now that had disappeared. He had a nice sloping forehead, a well-defined straight nose, a strong chin.

As if he sensed I was looking at him, he stiffened, and I quickly looked away. Everyone seemed mesmerized. Susie had nestled her head against Chuck's shoulder and closed her eyes. I let my heart lean into the music, and I drifted, soared, felt an inner comfort I hadn't felt before here.

This morning I'd been on the road; tonight I was hearing a world-famous singer perform just for us, so close I could touch her. All too soon Helena finished. I clapped until my palms hurt. Helena stood up and inclined her head, lowering her gaze modestly.

My headache was back; my ears felt plugged. I yawned.

"I can see my lullaby has made more than one person ready to sleep," Helena said, smiling at me.

"Yes. I think I'll call it a night. I'm thirsty," I said. "If someone will point me in the direction of the kitchen, I'll get a drink of water before I turn in."

"I'll show you," Rudy offered. "And then I'll take you to your room. Where are you stashing her, Jerry?"

"Number Three. It's just across from the lodge, so if you need anything at night, you're close."

"Uncle Jeremiah, please don't worry about me." I bent and kissed his forehead. I said good night to the other guests, nodded to Donovan, who returned my nod curtly, and followed Rudy.

The dining room was separated from the living room by a wide, short hall. There was a broad carved arch leading into a spacious dining room that had chalk-white walls, exposed dark-grained wood beams, and large picture windows. The two rectangular tables were already set up for breakfast.

Rudy pushed open a swinging door, and we entered the kitchen. "I'm not sure where the glasses are," he said.

"By the sink, I imagine." I opened the cupboard nearest me and discovered dozens of glasses as well as several bottles of prescription medicines and some aspirin. "Good. Just what I need," I said, pushing at the lid of the aspirin bottle with my thumb.

"You have to put the top on the arrow," Rudy said, watching me with unconcealed amusement.

"I did. It won't budge."

"Here, let me." Rudy dug his nails under and pulled. He twirled the top and twisted it, his face reddening with the effort. Scowling, he yanked open several drawers. "Ah, this ought to do it." He pulled out some pliers and wrenched off the top.

"It looks like Godzilla had a headache and helped himself," I said.

Rudy chuckled and poured a couple of aspirin into my outstretched hand.

I popped them into my mouth and washed them down with water. "I feel better already."

Rudy reached into a nearby bread box. "How about a muffin? I happen to know Lupita made some for dinner."

He handed me one and helped himself. Resting our hips against the counter, we stood in a companionable silence and ate.

"Why don't you and Donovan like each other?" I asked. Rudy seemed so likable it was hard to imagine anyone disliking him. Donovan was a different story. He was feisty, opinionated—although Uncle Jeremiah obviously thought he was great.

"We're from different worlds," Rudy answered in his straightforward, unabashedly honest way. "I like fast-moving, dirt-kicking bikes. Donovan is an ecology freak. Add to that the fact I'm leasing a few hundred acres of land in the foothills from Jerry, and you've got the problem. Donovan doesn't think the desert is big enough for both of us." Rudy took an angry bite of his muffin.

"I've been wondering about something. Is Donovan trying to buy Uncle Jeremiah's land?"

"I've been trying to figure that out myself," Rudy said. "I mean, the guy lives like a desert rat—camping down by the cottonwoods. I don't see where he'd have the money. But he talks like he's had money. He fits right in with the guests, while I have to fake it and usually end up blowing it."

"You wash your elbows in finger bowls, drink straight from the soup bowl."

Rudy grinned good-naturedly. "Something like that. Don't chew daintily. Probably would use the wrong fork. Although Jerry doesn't go much for style around here. The guests are supposed to be roughing it, experiencing the West like it was. Anyway, Jerry's keeping the bidding hush-hush, which is strange. He used to be a pretty open guy. So I don't know who I'm competing against. Of course, when he had his accident everything went on hold. So I don't really know what's going on. I figure I'll just keep a poker face and wait for the cards to fall."

"You said Donovan camps out? In what? A trailer?"

"No, nothing simple like that. He built a shelter out of—I don't know—dried cactus ribs, mesquite, mud. Looks like a pack rat's nest to me and about as comfortable."

"But why would he do something like that?"

Rudy shrugged. "He appeared about four months ago, talked to Jeremiah, and the next thing I know he's got a big say around here—mostly about what *I* shouldn't be allowed to do. And I was here first."

I thought about that for a minute. I hoped Donovan wasn't taking advantage of my uncle—freeloading, trying to con him out of the land.

"I've heard he used to be a science teacher in L.A., that he got fed up with city life," Rudy went on. "Now he's a granola-eating, back-to-nature guy."

A teacher? A dropout from society? A naturalist? No wonder he and Rudy were at odds. Two totally

different temperaments. "I guess that explains his uneven hair—cuts it himself probably." I was amused
and reluctantly impressed. "What does he live on?"

"Who knows?" Rudy rummaged around for some-
thing else to eat and finally settled on a third muffin.
"He does odd jobs for Jerry. Eats here sometimes.
Want some milk?"

"Sure." I wandered over to the large window, di-
gesting this new information. If he lived off the land,
no wonder Donovan was so rugged and lean looking.
However, I wasn't totally convinced that there wasn't
more to Donovan's apparently innocent, unmotivated,
sudden residence here. But I'd keep my suspicions to
myself. There seemed to be enough hard feelings between the two without my adding fuel—at least until I
was sure.

Outside the window, soft moonlight lit a clearing.
As I stared at the large boulders framing the space on
either end, I was startled to see a dark doglike shadow
appear, dragging what looked like a huge bone.

"Rudy, there's an animal out there."

"Probably just a coyote. Lupita puts leftovers out.
Sometimes when there are lots of guests, Jerry puts
the spotlight on this place so they can see the wildlife." Rudy handed me an icy glass of milk.

"You say that as if it doesn't matter. Don't forget
I'm a city girl. I find wild animals scary. I like them in
zoos or movies, not within touching distance."

"The most dangerous things around here are scor-
pions. Just remember to check your shoes in the
morning before you put them on, and you'll be okay.
And rattlers. Although it's a little cold for them yet."

I rinsed out the glass and put it on the drainboard to dry.

"Ready to see the cabin?" Rudy asked, walking to the back door.

I hung back. "What about the coyote?"

"It'll slink away when it hears us."

Even so, once we were outside, I glanced around nervously. Spots of moonlight outlined century plants neatly placed along a gravel path with tiny gas lanterns marking the way. As Uncle Jeremiah had promised, my Room 3, which was located in one of the cottages, was only about five hundred yards from the main building, and I felt very relieved.

Rudy put his hand on the doorknob, and the door swung open.

"In Chicago my door has three different locks," I said.

"Coyotes haven't mastered doors yet. Seriously, the guests are all from well-to-do backgrounds. The ranch is isolated enough to discourage strangers. And the wranglers take turns acting as night patrolmen in the early evening when the guests are at dinner. You can relax. It's perfectly safe."

The small light on the bedside table was lit, giving the room a rosy glow. Beyond the open window the black night seemed held at bay. The narrow single bed had the gaily striped bedspread turned down, revealing a snowy white pillow that looked awfully inviting.

"Anything I can get you before I leave?" Rudy asked.

"No. You've been wonderful. Thank you. I'm going to brush my teeth—" I stopped in midsentence. "I completely forgot. My suitcase is in the trunk of my car. I don't have a toothbrush or a nightgown. I don't have clothes for tomorrow. . . ."

"No problem. Give me the key. I'll get it."

I reached in my pocket and handed him the key chain. A wave of exhaustion hit me. "I'm not sure I can stay awake for you to bring it back," I said. "I'm really tired."

"If the light isn't on, I'll leave it on the doorstep."

"Okay. Thanks, Rudy. I appreciate all you've done."

"Glad to help out. See you soon." He gave a friendly wave and headed out into the night. I could hear the crunch of his boots on the gravel grow faint.

It almost felt like too much effort to go into the bathroom. But I did and washed the day's accumulation of dust off my face. On the way to bed my legs felt wobbly and my head strange. Something wasn't right. This was more than just tiredness. As I reached to draw the curtains, my hand couldn't seem to touch the cord. Every time I felt for it, the cord seemed to be somewhere else. The room was spinning. I lurched for the bed, feeling frightened, queasy, while slowly the periphery of my vision seemed to fold inward. A blackness came from the edges and swallowed me whole. . . .

CHAPTER THREE

My eyelids felt as if they had weights attached. I pushed them open, and slowly they sank shut. With effort I opened them again and stared into the white blur of a face only inches from mine.

"Oh, thank heavens! You're waking up."

When I tried to speak, my tongue was too thick, too heavy to move. Even swallowing was an effort. I was dimly aware of my head being lifted, my nose being squashed into the fabric of the person's shirt. For a frightening second I thought that I was going to suffocate and that I was too weak to resist. Then my nose was free and I was being pushed up. It was like coming to the surface after being flat on the bottom of the ocean.

"Try to sit up. They're getting coffee."

Sitting up was the last thing I felt like doing. Every cell in my body wanted to drift back into sleep, but before I knew it, my feet were dangling over the side of the bed, the tips of my toes brushing against the cool tile floor. A person whose name I knew I should

27

know and couldn't remember had an arm around my
waist, supporting me. The room was spinning so fast I
had to close my eyes to stop the nausea.

A door opened and slammed shut. "I made a whole
pot. How is she?"

"See for yourself." A cool hand cupped my chin,
tilting it up. A fingertip lightly lifted my right eyelid.
There were fingers on my pulse.

"I want you to open your eyes, Judith." The voice
shattered my fuzzy thoughts. This time it was a man's
voice. Strict. No-nonsense. "Drink this." There was
no choice, really. The rim of the cup was pressed
forcefully against my lips, which gave no resistance at
all. Hot liquid swirled into my mouth and too fast
down my throat. I choked.

"Be careful. She'll inhale it," a woman said.

"Judith, pay attention to what you're doing," the
male voice commanded.

"I know you," I tried to say, but the words were
washed away by a torrent of hot coffee.

"Can you manage now?" I didn't know if he was
speaking to me or to someone else. Disjointed words
appeared in my brain and then fogged over.

"I think so. Thank you."

His comment was lost in the bang of the door.

I don't know how many swallows I took before my
head got clearer, before I recognized Helena Knight
and Margot Hill. They alternated between making me
drink coffee and walking me around the small room.
When I got steadier, we moved outside and walked up
and down paths until finally my head was clear and
my gait even.

Finally I was allowed to go back inside. I lay down

gratefully. "I think you're going to be all right now." Helena, both hands on her hips, surveyed me with a critical eye.

"What happened?" My voice sounded unfamiliar—as if it belonged to a very small stranger.

"You passed out. As I was going by your room, I saw you lying on the floor. I got concerned when I couldn't rouse you. Donovan and Margot were still in the living room, so they helped me."

So the man had been Donovan. I might have known—all business, no sympathy.

"When I came into the room, I felt really strange—dizzy, disoriented, like I might be sick. I wonder. . . . Where's Rudy?"

"He came back with your suitcase," Helena said, "Donovan sent him away—he said you weren't feeling well but that things were under control. Now"—she sat down beside me and took my cold hand in her warm one—"what did you take to give you a reaction like that?"

"Take?" It took me a second to realize she thought I'd overdosed on some kind of sleeping medication.

"I didn't take anything." I paused. "Except some aspirin."

"Honey, no aspirin in the world would knock you out like that."

"That's the only thing I took." Mentally I went over the evening. I'd stopped for a hamburger at some little town on my way to the ranch. I'd had milk and muffins in the kitchen, but so had Rudy. The only thing I'd done besides that was take the aspirin.

My thoughts and words were coming more easily now.

"She's all right," Margot said. "We can leave now."

Helena looked uncertain.

"Yes," I said. "It's late. I'm sorry to have been a problem. I'll be fine. Thanks for noticing . . . for doing something."

"I'm in Room 8," Helena said. "It's two cottages down. If you feel ill during the night, come and get me. Or you can get Margot."

"I'm in the main building—the small room next to the office. It doesn't cost as much as the others," Margot added.

"Thank you both," I said again.

After the door closed behind them, I lay awake for a while, trying to make sense of everything, couldn't, and fell into a deep sleep.

I woke with a start, disoriented and shaky. It took me a moment to remember where I was and why I was in bed wearing my clothes. I'd been dreaming of home, of my cozy bedroom with its tiny rose-patterned wallpaper, of the pale-pink velvet-cushioned window seat over Lakeland Avenue, where I still like to curl up on a free afternoon and read.

At home, lying in bed in the morning, I could hear the buzz of traffic on the street below, the morning church bells from St. Andrews on the corner, and the early-morning delivery trucks emptying their wares at Baldacci's grocery two doors down. Here there was total silence. All I could hear was my own breathing.

Getting up, I went to the window and pulled back the curtain. It was barely dawn outside. In the distance, silhouetted against an opal sky, was the outline of a huge, stark mountain. I knew at once that must be the infamous Silver Dome that Mom had talked about forever. It was home to a defunct silver mine, a ghost town. But instead of finding it fascinating, I had a sudden surge of homesickness—a gut wondering of what in the world I was doing here. I still wasn't feeling very well, and it was doing a number on my self-confidence, I thought. After a shower and a jog maybe my head would clear and my confidence come back.

When I opened my suitcase after my shower, I was surprised and more than a little annoyed to see all the contents jumbled. I'd packed so carefully. I could see Rudy with the suitcase slung over his shoulder, racing through the desert on his ATV. No wonder. For all I knew, he might have carried it upside down.

I pulled out a pair of navy shorts and the top of my blue velour jogging suit. It was undoubtedly too warm for the pants. I glanced from the closet to the suitcase...I should unpack. No, it felt like too much effort.

Although it was cool outside, a smell in the air promised heat. The sky was almost gold now, the mountains a royal purple. Everywhere I looked there were cacti—some tall and majestic, others short, round, prickly. Each one as it was highlighted by the rising sun had a stark beauty. There weren't any human noises, but birds chattered. All around were wooden bird feeders filled to overflowing with bird-seed.

On a tiny patch of green lawn in front of the main lodge were eight or nine soft rock-colored bunnies complete with cotton-puff tails. Cottontails—the kind of rabbit every little girl dreams of picking up and cuddling. I crouched, enchanted. One lifted its head, its tiny nose quivering, and regarded me with perfect round, bright black eyes.

Not wanting to scare them, I walked out of sight before I began my stretching exercises preparatory to jogging. I bent my right knee and put my left leg straight out behind me as far back as it would go, then alternated. My head was feeling better. I found myself wondering if maybe the combination of sheer exhaustion and worry, on top of the aspirin, had acted in such a way that it had zonked me. Or else I'd had a touch of some quick, violent flu.

I couldn't shake the feeling that someone was watching me. But whenever I turned, no one was there. In fact, no one else seemed to be up. The little cottages surrounded by cacti and a handful of mesquite trees had their curtains drawn. They were painted a playful pink and had bright Mexican tiles with painted numbers surrounded by swirling flowers.

I jogged down the dirt road leading away from the ranch, past a corral with a dozen or more horses pulling clumps of what looked like hay from compressed stacks. A black horse lifted its head and whinnied at me. Beautiful as it was, I'd preferred the cottontails. My best friend as a girl had loved horses, and I'd pretended the same interest, but secretly I was afraid of them. They seemed huge, uncontrollable. If I had to ride something around here, I'd vote for Rudy's ATV.

When I came to a sandy riverbed—wash, Mom had told me they were called—I decided to see where it led. As long as I kept the water tower of the ranch in sight, I'd be okay. The sand in the wash was fairly thick and pulled at my tendons and muscles. It didn't take long before my calves were aching.

As I slowed down, a tantalizing aroma filtered through the thick brush, but I wasn't sure which direction it was coming from. Ahead of me the wash spread out in a fork, one wider than the other. A fairly wide but shallow stream of water ran down the center. The banks of the wash were steeper here, and large, flat gray rocks were stacked on its edge as if by a playful giant.

Huge sycamores and eucalyptus trees grew alongside brush I didn't recognize. There was a grove of cottonwoods. That had been Mom's favorite place to play—because it was cooler. To me, the trees made everything seem gloomy. Globs of what looked like a woman's hair, but which I decided must be some kind of moss, hung from the high branches. Even though there were some picnic tables scattered under the trees, I found it unnerving and caught myself looking over my shoulder, as if I expected someone to be following me or to pop out from behind a tree.

I turned around and went back out into the sunlight, choosing the other dry fork of the wash. Soon I could hear the unmistakable sizzle of a fire. As I rounded the corner, there was Donovan. He was in a clearing, his back to me, squatting on his haunches, all his attention focused on a small, smoky fire. He was frying something that smelled so good, my stomach growled. Either he heard my footsteps or my stomach because he suddenly jumped to his feet and whirled around, fists clenched. I stopped dead in my tracks.

"Oh, it's you." He loosened his large hands and rubbed them against his faded, patched jeans.

"Well, good morning to you too," I answered.

He was wearing his usual expression—a frown. He came closer, peering at me. "Are you okay?"

"Okay? Oh, you mean because of last night."

He looked at me as if I'd lost my mind. "Passing out is a nightly occurrence? It doesn't even rattle you?" The frown deepened.

"Of course it rattled me. I don't know what happened. The only drug I took was some aspirin I found in the kitchen at the ranch."

"Are you sure you took aspirin? Is it possible you made a mistake?"

I shook my head. "It was aspirin. I had trouble with the childproof cap. Rudy helped me— Wait a minute. I didn't even look at the tablets. I just assumed. Obviously, unconsciously they *felt* the right size, so I just swallowed them. How stupid! I guess they could have been anything . . . maybe aspirin and codeine."

"And meant for Jeremiah to take, not you," Donovan muttered. "With his flare-up of emphysema, if he'd taken them instead of you, it could have seriously hurt him—maybe even killed him. That would depress his breathing even further."

"Why would anyone want to hurt Uncle Jeremiah?"

Donovan looked at me, started to speak, and then caught his lower lip between his teeth. His eyes behind the wire frame of his glasses were cloudy, unsure. He glanced around and motioned me closer, as if he suspected someone might overhear. "I'm beginning to think Jeremiah's accidents may not be accidents."

"The fall?"

"He didn't fall. I think someone pushed the ladder out from under him. There was that other accident, too, you know. A year or so ago when he nearly fell down a dry-well shaft. Now this—this accidental in-gesting of an obviously potent drug, hidden in an aspirin bottle."

"Look, I don't know if that's what happened," I said, beginning to feel anxious at his assumptions. "It may have been a virus. I know I was exhausted. When I go back to the ranch, I'll snag the bottle. We can examine it more closely."

"Good idea. But, Judith, let's keep our findings to ourselves. If there is someone out there trying to hurt your uncle, we don't want him or her to know we know."

"I agree." I wrinkled my nose, something catching my attention. "Donovan, your food is burning."

With surprising agility Donovan leaped to the fire and grabbed the pan, passing it from one hand to the other until he could reach a cloth sacking and wrap it around the handle. He poked at the contents with a fork. "Saved in time." He flipped whatever it was over and replaced the pan over the fire.

"Fish?" I asked. I moved in closer. "Fresh trout? But where . . . out here. . . ."

"There's a stocked pond over there, beyond the sec-ond row of cottonwoods."

"I love trout." I smiled at him and crouched near the fire. If he thought I was leaving without having been offered at least a bite, he was in for a surprise.

He read my mind. "There are only two, and they aren't very big."

"If you'll lend me your pole, I'll try my hand. I fish all the time with my brothers."

"I'm afraid you'd have trouble. My flytying isn't

the best. They keep slipping off. I nearly lost one of these. I fell in, trying to grab him before he got away. If you'd been two seconds earlier, you'd have caught me in an embarrassing situation."

Sure enough, a pair of jeans, shorts, and a blue shirt hung from the spiny branches of a nearby mesquite.

"You might have been embarrassed. I wouldn't have. I'm used to seeing people undressed. It's part of my job. I wouldn't have thought twice about it," I told him.

He'd lifted the frying pan off the piece of tin he'd constructed over the flame, and in a practiced maneuver put a blue-speckled coffeepot in its place. As he bent over the pan, his hair flopped across his forehead. It was beautiful hair, thick and naturally streaked with a dozen different shades from blond to a deep auburn. He cut the fish into equal parts, grabbed a plate and what looked like the lid of a coffee can. "Heads or tails?"

"No eyes."

He cut the fish in half—fairly. He handed me the tail ends served on the lid. "Sorry, I've got only one of everything. I get the fork and you the spoon. I'm not used to entertaining."

I looked around and saw a nearby flat rock that looked perfect for sitting.

"Wait— Never mind. It moved."

I jumped up, my trout sliding precariously near the edge of my lid. "What moved?"

"You nearly sat on a horned toad sunning. There it goes." He pointed to a dirt-colored lump that scurried under another rock. "You do have to watch your step around here. I have a number of friends who drop in for unexpected visits. There are a couple of ground squirrels that stop by for raisins and nuts. A cottontail that's partial to carrot tops. And every so often a quail. She had a broken wing. I patched her up."

"Like a Dr. Doolittle of the desert."

"I guess so."

"I hope if the horned lizard had been a rattler I'd have noticed it. I know how to dodge taxis, but I'm a novice about the desert, and I'm scared to death of snakes and spiders."

"Maybe I can raise your consciousness about spiders. Most of them are harmless. Actually, rattlers are fairly shy. I haven't found one in my campground yet. But if you do much tromping around in the desert, I'd suggest boots, not tennis shoes. Ankles are the main hit spots."

"I'll remember that." I sat down carefully, balancing the lid on my knees. I took a small bite of the fish. "This is delicious."

"I've gotten to be a pretty good cook. In the beginning I came close to starving to death. One day all I had to eat was a prickly-pear-cactus fruit." He cut his fish into five neat pieces and speared one with his fork. "I guess you're wondering what I'm doing here."

His eyes skimmed me once, then again. They were a clear hazel—the kind of rapidly changing color that made me think of a high mountain stream rushing over multicolored pebbles, but so clear you could see every single detail. With Donovan, when his eyes weren't obscured by a frown, his gaze was so clear and simple I felt as if I could see every thought passing.

"I am curious," I admitted. "You don't exactly seem like the mountain-man type."

He poured some remarkably strong coffee, complete with grounds in the bottom—cowboy coffee, he called it—into a dented cup and an old soup can.

This time he gave me the cup. He settled down near me, his back against a rock, his long legs crossed at the ankles. "Looks like you've taught yourself to sew," I said, looking at the patches on his jeans. I was amazed that a man could do such neat, even stitches. I couldn't.

"It took some doing," he said, flushing slightly. He shifted his weight and put his legs farther away from mine, curling them under. "I'm too tall to sit comfortably like this for very long." Resting the cup in his lap, he told me in more detail what Rudy had alluded to last night. Born and raised in L.A., he'd taught freshman biology classes for seven years, lived in a crowded apartment complex, traveled in rush-hour traffic to and from his job, and generally lived a tense, hectic life. One weekend he decided to show his class what it was like to camp out in the desert.

"There was something about the total peace of lying in a sleeping bag out under the stars that really made an impression on me. But the other thing that shook me was that everywhere I looked, there were traces of civilization: plastic wrappers, aluminum cans. After I got back I decided I wanted to live in the wilds somewhere by my own wits. My idea was to live by and with whatever the desert had to offer."

"You're using cans," I said. "So you didn't give up material things completely."

"I know. I had to give up on some of my ideals. But slowly I'm using less."

"I didn't mean to interrupt you. Go on."

"So I took a year's leave of absence. I tried the Mojave Desert, but there were too many silver trailers and campgrounds filled with Midwesterners, dirt bikes, dune buggies, and all-terrain vehicles. Gradually I worked my way here. Then. . . ." He paused. "Someone told me about Jeremiah's place. So I came here and fell in love with it."

"Are you one of the potential buyers?" I asked, unable to let the chance for some information pass.

He gazed at me shrewdly. "It's crossed my mind. But if I did, what would I do with it?"

"And it would cost a lot of money. How does a schoolteacher, a back-to-nature guy, have funding like that?"

He laughed. "You're direct, aren't you?"

"Yes. Feel free to tell me it's none of my business."

"Okay, it's none of your business, but I'll tell you anyway. I lived very frugally in L.A., *and*—a big *and*—my grandmother left me a nice trust fund. I could buy the land, but maintaining it would be a problem, and since I wouldn't know what I wanted to do with it, other than return it to its natural state, that would cause a problem too. So I haven't actually bid on the place. However, I know I don't want someone like Rudy to buy it. I'd rather fork over everything I have to prevent that."

"Rudy seems like a nice guy."

A look of outrage passed over Donovan's fine features. "Have you seen what those things he and his buddies ride do to the desert? Have you *seen* the destruction, heard the noise pollution? Not to mention the fact that they're dangerous. Ask him sometime how many injuries happen, how many people lose their lives or are maimed. . . ."

I flinched. I'd seen what happened when you rode a motorcycle into a car. I'd worked with brain-damaged kids, kids who'd lost an arm or a leg, kids who were paraplegics as the result of a motorcycle accident.

"I see your point," I said softly. "Well, I don't know what the solution to the ranch is. It's a shame Uncle Jeremiah has to sell it at all. Even though Mom hopes he'll come back with me, I know deep in her heart she wishes he'd stay right here—that nothing would ever change."

"Maybe you can talk him into doing that."

I glanced up in surprise—that hadn't occurred to me.

"I don't want you to think I'm sponging off your uncle," he added. "I do things around the ranch that need doing."

"I'm sure you do." I glanced around at the primitive lean-to, at his pants drying. Imagine staying here day after day. I'd freak out. I needed activity, action, other people. "How do you keep yourself occupied during the day?" I was sure constructing the hovel of twigs and mud or whatever it was had taken a long time. He had stacks of dead cacti and branches of trees. There were black strips of plastic stretched over a frame of mesquite. I realized his gaze was following mine and that he was smiling at my obvious lack of understanding how anyone could find living like this fun.

"I gather dead cactus and mesquite for the fire, which takes an amazing amount of time. I'm working on a solar system to heat my water." He jerked his head in the direction of the black plastic. A lock of his shaggy hair fell over his forehead. The sun caught the red tints and brightened the gold. *A woman would kill for such hair,* I thought.

"Going back to nature is hard in some respects," he admitted, "but awfully rewarding in others. I'm still not sure exactly what I'm searching for. But whatever it is, I'm determined not to wake up someday and discover twenty years have passed and I'm forty-nine and still running like a rat in a maze. . . ."

So he was twenty-nine. Four years older than I was. Was he older or younger than Rudy? Older probably.

"Why are you looking at me like that?"

"Like what?" I said, embarrassed at being caught even thinking about Rudy in his presence.

"Your eyes got a faraway, dreamy look. They're very interesting eyes. I like how when you look up there's a fine line of white underneath the iris. It makes you look—" He shrugged. "I don't know, innocent maybe. I'm not much with words. I'm more an idea man. Anyway, what were you thinking?"

"I was thinking about your age—how I have a brother a year younger and you remind me of him."

"The one who takes you fishing?"

"No." I laughed. "The one who takes me fishing is Eddie—he's as bouncy as a rubber ball and nine years old."

"Just how many brothers do you have?"

"Four. I'm sandwiched in the middle."

"You're one of five children?"

"My mom is a *mom,*" I said. "Her only sister died when they were children. So she grew up wanting lots of kids. How about you? Any brothers or sisters?"

He shook his head. "No. I can identify with your mother. I'm an only child."

"My secret wish all my life," I joked. "In fact, I wanted to be an only child so badly that for my tenth birthday, my dad stripped the upstairs hall closet, painted it bright red, made a little desk and a small bookcase, and even ran electricity into it so that I could have a playroom just for me. I'd hide in there and read to my heart's content. My brothers were forbidden to enter it. Which, of course, they did all the time secretly and not so secretly to tease me. They'd leave notes signed *The Phantom*—things like that."

"That would have appealed to me too. I wasn't into sports. I read, did puzzles, figured things out."

"I can see you," I teased gently, aware that I was liking him more and more, "sitting curled up in a chair, wearing tiny wire-rimmed glasses, your head bent over a book."

"A nerd, in other words?"

"Oh no, I didn't mean it like that at all," I said, horrified that he thought I was making fun of him. "It sounds like you had a wonderful childhood—all that love and attention."

"It was lonely," he admitted. "I missed having a father." He tipped his shoulders back and, closing his eyes, leaned his face so that the sun fell fully upon it. "Jeremiah has kind of filled that role for me since I've been here."

"That's nice." I tried to imagine my childhood

without Dad and couldn't. I used to kneel on the living-room couch, my nose pressed against the front window, watching for him to walk up the sidewalk. I'd meet him at the door, arms lifted to be swung in the air, then held against his shoulder where I'd feel the roughness of his chin against my cheek. "I guess having the ranch nearby makes living like this less lonely," I said, stopping the memories and returning to the present.

"I'm not lonely here," he corrected. "I feel totally in tune with the surroundings and nature. When the ranch sells, I may not be able to face going back. Maybe I'll just retreat farther and farther away from civilization until I'm huddled in a cave somewhere up in Silver Dome, observing the land, writing in my journal. . . ."

"How about the kids you taught? Don't you miss them?"

"Actually, I do. A couple of them write."

"How do you get mail here?"

"I cheat." He grinned—a wide-open grin. "I have my mail sent in care of the ranch. A concession to my mother . . . and to Holly."

"Holly?"

"My girlfriend."

CHAPTER FOUR

*G*irlfriend. He had a girlfriend? I felt as if I'd been punched in the stomach, as if I'd had the air knocked out of me. I averted my gaze so he wouldn't see the surprise and shock that I knew must be etched on my face. When I looked at him again, he was busy dumping coffee grounds onto the ground. "Your girl-friend doesn't care that you've just gone off into the wilderness?" I said, faking a nonchalance I didn't feel. "She must be an amazingly tolerant woman."

"Holly? Tolerant?" He gave a hollow laugh. "Be-lieve me, that word isn't in her vocabulary." He got to his feet and held out his hand to take my coffee cup.

I handed it to him. Why should the revelation that Donovan had a girlfriend upset me? True, I'd felt a slight attraction, a *very slight* attraction. Certainly a perfectly manageable feeling. I'd sworn, after Kevin, I wouldn't be interested in another guy for a long, long time. So the fact that he had a girlfriend shouldn't matter at all. But it did.

Donovan scuffed some dirt onto the fire, to put it

45

out, and didn't volunteer any more information. The silence between us grew.

With effort I swallowed back a couple of questions. I could ask him about his interest in the ranch, but even I knew that prying into his love life was none of my business. If anybody pried into mine, I'd have a fit. I hadn't even told Mom the whole story of my breakup with Kevin. And I told her almost everything.

Even in my work one of the first things I'd learned in dealing with my patients was that everybody needed to divulge painful past experiences at his own pace. Since I wasn't ready to talk about Kevin, I had to assume, even if Donovan's relationship with his girlfriend was okay, that I had no right to ask questions.

"I understand breakfast is served promptly at eight," I said, steering myself into an innocuous subject.

"You'll hear Lupita ring the triangle—a fifteen-minute warning, then the real thing."

"Schedules. I thought that's what guests came here to avoid."

"Not completely. When you run a resort, you have to have certain rules. Otherwise people would sleep until noon and nothing would get done. What's relaxing is the lack of noise—no phones ringing, only one small TV, things like that."

I stood up and threw my hands up in the air, stretching with a catlike contentment. "I enjoyed my prebreakfast snack. Thanks."

There was a pop, a streaking whine, and something passed so close to my cheek I felt my hair lift. Behind me came the sound of a dull thud. The next thing I knew, Donovan had hurled himself through the air, his body hitting mine. He knocked me to the ground beneath him. There was dust in my eyes, dirt in my mouth. He felt incredibly heavy.

"Get off! You're hurting me!" I wiggled, shoving at him with my free arm and squirming to free up my legs.

"Lie still! Someone took a shot at us." He shifted to one side, his arm still across my waist, as if he didn't trust that I wouldn't stand up.

Was that what it was? All around us there was absolute silence. My own heart was ticking like a bomb about to go off. I could feel the tautness of Donovan's muscles, hear each intake of breath. He kept his head low, while his narrowed eyes searched the surrounding growth like radar. His chin was inches from my mouth; I could see the rough shaving job he had done as well as a faint half moon of a childhood scar.

"I'm going to move my arm," Donovan said after a few minutes, "and I'm going to sit up. If nothing happens, I want you to inch behind that rock over there so that you're protected while I look around."

"I want to go with you."

"It isn't safe."

"It'll be okay. I can take care of myself."

"Do you ever do what anybody tells you to do?" he asked, sounding more bewildered than annoyed.

"Rarely." I pushed his arm off but I didn't sit up. I lay there, aware of the hardness of the ground, the silence. Everything Donovan had warned me about earlier rushed through my mind at once. How the ladder tipping over hadn't been an accident. The story about the well. How I'd taken a drug obviously intended for my uncle.

I realized Donovan had risen to a crouch position. He stood, shoulders kind of hunched as if to protect his neck. Slowly I got to my feet, imitating his posture. My body was braced, half expecting another shot. Ripples of fear like sprinkles of cold water spread across my skin. I was ready to fling myself on the ground if I heard so much as a twig snap.

There were no more gunshots, no noises whatsoever. As I felt Donovan relax, I did too. I bent over and examined my knees. Both were scraped and bleeding.

"Look over there. Look at that cactus."

I followed Donovan's hand. Less than ten feet behind us one of the arms of a giant saguaro cactus had been hit dead center and splintered in half. It was a sobering sight. If the shot had hit either one of us— Instinctively I put my hands up and felt my head, the sleekness of my long hair, my cheeks, my neck. "Maybe we should call the police." A long, trembling shudder swallowed up my last few words.

Donovan looked thoughtful. "I suppose we could call the sheriff. But we have no proof. He could say someone was target shooting. Unfortunately, all kinds of people pack guns out here."

"They do at home too."

"Do you hear what I hear?" Donovan held up both hands.

In the distance there was the low rumble of an engine. Before I could answer, Donovan took off in a sprint in the direction of the sound. I followed, running lightly, easily, in spite of my stinging knees.

Donovan flashed me an annoyed look over his shoulder.

"You stay here."

"No. I'm not going to be left behind."

"Judith!"

"Save your breath," I retorted. "I'm going wherever you go."

Running through the desert took concentration. The ground was uneven, and there were holes, splits in the land that ranged from a few inches to a few feet. And, of course, there were a thousand cacti to dodge. The brush tore at my legs and arms. Branches swiped at my face.

Donovan didn't seem to know a runner's secret of pacing. After a few minutes he was panting, and I, while warm, wasn't even out of breath. We climbed a slight rise, and Donovan stopped so suddenly I nearly ran into him. Ahead of us was a cloud of dust. It was an ATV, but it was so far away it was impossible to make out the rider. Donovan turned to face me. His face was bright red and streaked with dirt from our fall. Rivulets of sweat trickled down his cheeks. His glasses were askew. "Rudy," he said. "I'll bet you anything that's him."

"Rudy? Are you crazy? Rudy wouldn't shoot at us. At least he wouldn't shoot at me. You, I'm not so sure."

"He wants this land. I don't think he cares how he gets it."

"You really think he'd try to kill Uncle Jeremiah?" I stared at Donovan in disbelief.

"Somebody's trying to. It wouldn't surprise me to find out it's Rudy. He knows I'm against Jeremiah's selling out to him, and it rankles. Now you're here. He's probably really worried. Worried enough that he's going to try more openly."

"This isn't making sense, Donovan. Do you really think Rudy would shoot, miss, and then go riding off on an ATV in plain sight? If Rudy were guilty, and I'm sure he isn't, I think he'd be more subtle."

"Maybe. . . ." Donovan didn't sound convinced.

"Or if he shot once and missed, why wouldn't he shoot again until he hit us? And the two incidents could be entirely unrelated. Whoever shot at us could be hiding in the bush. The person on the ATV could be out riding for fun."

"Unlikely but possible." Donovan ran his fingers through his hair, which had flopped over his forehead. He was still breathing heavily although he tried to hide it.

"I'm going riding later today with Rudy. That will give me a chance to do some poking around. Maybe I can find out who was on the ATV this morning. Maybe I can uncover some useful information."

"You're going riding? On one of those things?"

"Just for a little while. Don't worry, I'll be careful."

Donovan's face had clouded over.

"If I backed out after all he's done for me, it would be rude. I'll just go once. I'll have my antenna up. If I sense anything wrong, I won't go again," I said.

"So, in spite of everything I've told you about the destructiveness of those things, you're going to ride one, anyway."

"I should have known it wasn't worry over me or my safety that concerned you." I felt a tiny flash of annoyance that he didn't give me any credit for bravery or for intelligence. "You're just put out because I won't follow *your* crusade like a blind recruit."

Donovan didn't argue. The disapproval, annoyance, or whatever unpleasant expression he'd conjured up moments ago had left. His face was stoical, a mask of sharp lines and firmness.

I suppose I could have admitted that I had my reservations about ATVs, that I knew what damage they could inflict on humans, that I hadn't liked the knocked-down cacti, the rutted trails I'd seen yesterday. Instead, I heard myself continue in the opposite direction. "I had fun last night. Maybe *you* should ride an ATV sometime. You might change your mind."

"The day I get on an ATV—"

"Careful. I've noticed whenever I make a flat statement like you're about to make, it ends up happening."

"I can promise you that I will *never, ever* ride an ATV."

We stood facing each other, locked in a stalemate staring contest. I thought of how many times one of my brothers and I found ourselves in this silly state, unable, even as adults, to give up, to break the stare first.

It was hard to keep a straight face. I felt like sticking out my tongue or crossing my eyes, just to see what his reaction would be. I'd outrun him. Maybe I should give in, I thought after a few more seconds. I was a champion in our family. I could outstare anybody. As an only child Donovan couldn't have had the experience I had. I waited a few more seconds, then blinked and looked away.

Where were we, anyway? While we'd been running, I hadn't paid attention. As I looked around, I realized I didn't know north from south, east from west. Nothing seemed familiar. In the direction the ATV had gone, there were foothills that led up to a high, rugged, unfriendly-looking mountain. Silver Dome—that was the name Mom had told me.

I glanced at Donovan, hating to admit to him, of all people, that I didn't know where I was. "How do I get back to the ranch?" I asked finally.

"I'll take you."

"There's no need. If you'll just point the way, I can find it myself."

"*I'll* escort you."

We tramped in silence through the scrub. Several times Donovan held a branch aside for me. Soon we were on what looked like a riding trail—there were hoofprints and horse droppings. A trickle of blood from my knee had reached my sock.

"I see the water tower. I know where I am now," I said.

Donovan didn't answer—he kept right on walking.

I saw a flash of blue material out of the corner of my eye. I stopped and stared into the brush. Someone was over there.

"Donovan," I said softly. "Wait."

But he didn't hear. He continued to stalk ahead of me. I'd waited just long enough that I was going to be seen by whoever it was if I didn't do something and quick. It wasn't until I was behind a large five-armed saguaro cactus that I realized that this morning's events had made me slightly paranoid. Undoubtedly whoever was tromping through the brush had a perfectly good reason for being there. We were near the ranch, after all. Still, I remained frozen in my hiding place, every cell alert for danger as the crunch of boots on hard-packed dirt came closer.

I pressed my hand against my lips as Helena Knight came into view. She was wearing a bright-blue long-sleeved blouse. There was a band of red-braided rope around her waist, and her striped baggy pants were caught just under the knees by polished English riding boots. Her outfit was colorful, pretty. But what really blew my mind was the fact that in her right hand, not concealed from sight at all, was a small pearl-handled gun.

My glance flew from the gun up to Helena's face. She was staring at the ground, looking this way and that—for footprints, I immediately thought. My heart was hammering so loudly I was afraid if she paused, she'd hear it. Her expression was frighteningly severe.

She was past me in seconds. Thank heavens her path didn't follow Donovan's. I waited until she was out of sight and then scurried after Donovan, thinking that by now he'd have noticed I wasn't behind him and would be waiting. The cottages of the ranch popped into view. A setting of complete tranquility. Donovan was nowhere in sight.

Chuck Orsini appeared on the porch of a cottage. He was dressed in slacks and a yellow shirt. An elderly man using a cane to support himself hobbled off another porch and down onto the path ahead of me. I ran past them, past the normality of their morning and their greeting, locked in my own troubled mind.

Reaching my room, I washed my face and hands,

as if the cold water would calm my seething brain. I was trembling. Had Helena tried to shoot us? Why? It didn't make sense. Surely she hadn't brought me back from unconsciousness last night only to shoot me today. Try as I might, I couldn't make her into a villain. Besides, if she'd just taken a shot at me, wouldn't she at least have hidden the gun?

On the other hand, she had no idea I was there. If she'd come across Donovan and me, she could have slipped the gun into a pocket and we'd never have suspected a thing. . . . A rough knock on the cottage door almost made me jump out of my skin.

There was Donovan, his face pressed against the screen door, peering in.

"You scared me out of my wits. Where did you go?" I questioned, letting him in. "Didn't you hear me calling to you?"

He wrinkled his brow, regarding me with serious, clear eyes.

I didn't give him time to answer. "It was Helena!" I burst out. "I saw her. She was walking through the desert. She had a gun. I tried to tell you, but you'd gone on ahead. She could have shot us." I was aware I was babbling, but I couldn't stop.

Donovan took me by both upper arms and shook me gently. "Judith, Judith, it's okay. It wasn't Helena."

"How do you know? I saw *her*. She had a gun!"

"Helena always carries a gun. A little pearl-handled revolver. Her snake gun, she calls it."

"But couldn't that—"

Donovan shook his head. "No. It's a toy. A joke. Whatever hit that cactus was big time."

I stared at him, wanting to believe, but there'd been something about Helena's expression and seeing the gun. . . . It was hard to brush that aside.

"I got these for you." Donovan held up two Band-Aids. "For your knees."

When I didn't react, he took the paper off a Band-Aid and, bending over, put it carefully on my right knee, smoothing the ends to be sure that the whole wound was covered and that the Band-Aid stuck. It was a tender, careful gesture—a gesture only moments ago I would have thought beyond him.

He ripped open the next Band-Aid and repeated the procedure on my other knee.

I looked down. Visions of roller-skating accidents, playing softball, falling down, skipped through my mind. I'd had scabby knees during most of my rough-and-tumble childhood. I took a deep breath. Slowly the fear I'd been feeling disappeared. "Thank you."

"Listen, I've been thinking. When you go to breakfast, don't say anything about the shooting incident. Let's keep it to ourselves. And get the aspirin bottle. I couldn't find it."

"Did you look in the glass cabinet by the sink?"

"Yes. It wasn't there."

The gong sounded. I wondered briefly if it were the first or the second and decided I didn't care. They could start breakfast without me. "Are you staying for breakfast?"

"No, I can't. I've got something I have to do. Besides, I have some ethics. If I eat three meals a day here, I might as well stay in a cottage and get all duded up. I might be tempted to forget my experiment."

"I suppose you have a point."

"Judith." His voice was serious. "At breakfast—in fact, at all meals—keep your eyes open. Don't eat *anything* other people aren't eating."

"Okay."

"You know, from the moment I first saw you last night, the strangest feelings have been jiggling around inside me," he said suddenly. "Feelings I *don't* want to have. And yet I can't seem to stop."

"What feelings?" My question was soft, breathless sounding. I was aware that some icy place inside my own heart had melted, leaving me wondering, wanting, caring, needing to know more about what he was feeling. Because I thought I was feeling it too.

"I don't know. You sound so self-assured sometimes, so tough, and yet I see and feel a vulnerability that touches my heart, my protectiveness. The ridiculous part is that I don't even know you. The scientist part of me knows that doesn't make sense . . . the male part simply doesn't care. You're an intriguing woman, Judith Nelson."

He put his hand out, his fingers lightly touching my lips, then moving to stroke my cheek. I was dimly aware of his head moving toward me. *He's going to kiss me,* I thought, amazed and yet aware that I wanted him to. But just before I closed my eyes, I thought of Holly. Just the idea of her loomed dark and forbidding in the back of my mind. If he had a girlfriend, he had no business kissing me. Just because he'd chosen to live alone in the desert without her didn't mean I was willing to be some fill-in.

I moved my head; his lips caught the edge of my hair. I pulled away from his embrace and looked into his face. "I seem to remember an earlier conversation about a girlfriend," I said hoarsely.

"Did I forget to mention she's my ex-girlfriend?"

"Yes. No—I mean, you left that detail out."

"Well, she is. She broke up with me months ago. It turns out she found someone more her type—a stockbroker with lots of money, one who likes parties and stays in five-star hotels when he travels, not in a sleeping bag—that's a direct quote from her Dear Donovan letter."

Donovan's hands were around my waist. I looked into his eyes, aware that they were warm and filled with an intensity that struck a matching longing in me.

The weight of my body pushed forward until I was standing on tiptoes, my hands linked behind Donovan's neck, his hair brushing ever so gently against their backs. My lips rose to meet his. . . .

"So you *are* here," a voice called through the screen.

Donovan's hands slipped away from my waist. I jerked away from him, a hot flush filling my cheeks.

It was Margot. "We're all waiting breakfast on you, Judith," she said, peering through the screen at us. "Helena sent me to be sure you were all right."

"I'm sorry. I didn't realize the second bell had rung."

"I have to be going, anyway," Donovan said quietly. "I'll see you later."

"Donovan!"

He turned.

"Thanks . . . for the Band-Aids. For everything."

He smiled. A lovely smile that lit up his eyes and

creased his lean cheeks. "My pleasure." Then he was
through the door. I could see him nod to Margot.

I took a quick breath. Hot, flustered, my heart
beating like a hummingbird's wings, I pushed my hair
back and went outside, knowing that anyone could
look at me and see my flushed cheeks and my overly
bright eyes and know just exactly how the last few
moments with Donovan had excited me. For the first
time in months I felt snapped into place. Alive. As if
the shadowy presence of Kevin and the disappointment over our relationship that hadn't worked out was
finally finished. I hadn't lost all feeling. My heart was
in perfect working order and ready to trust again.

CHAPTER FIVE

There was no doubt that Margot had read my expression and added up correctly what she'd interrupted and that she didn't approve. A flurry of emotions passed quickly over her thin face, leaving her high cheekbones as flushed as my hot skin felt. Or was it jealousy? Had my appearance at the ranch fouled up some interest she'd had in Donovan? Oh, well, I couldn't worry about it. If she had a problem with how I conducted myself, it was exactly that—her problem.

A sea of faces stared at me as I entered the dining room. I tried to link the names with individuals. A few connected. I did notice immediately that Uncle Jeremiah wasn't among those seated. "There's a place for you between me and Helena," Margot said.

"Where's Uncle Jeremiah?" A niggling feeling of alarm wanted to push through the rosy glow enveloping me.

"He's not well. He's staying in his room."

"Don't worry, Judith. He's done this before and

always emerges looking and feeling better," Helena spoke up, as if sensing my concern. "I did check with Lupita. He's asked for meal trays, so he's eating." Her gaze left my face, taking in my jogging outfit and coming to rest on my bandaged knees. "What in the world happened to your poor legs?"

Her question made the temporary glow disappear. I remembered the sound of the gunshot and the fear I had felt. "I fell down when someone took a shot at me."

All conversation stopped.

Helena pressed her fingers on either side of her face, her eyes round, her mouth open. Either she was an awfully good actress, or she was genuinely shocked. "Someone shot at you?" she repeated.

"At me . . . or Donovan," I added. "I was at Donovan's place." Something powerful was at work inside me. I couldn't have stopped my words if I'd tried. Anger, fear—something—kept bubbling up. "And I want whoever did it, if that person is in this room, to know that I'm not scared." Not exactly the truth—my stomach was turning flip-flops.

A pleasant-looking Mexican woman—Lupita, I guessed—came through the swinging door, balancing a huge tray of cantaloupe slices filled with strawberries. She held the door open with a deft jutting of her hip so that a dark-eyed little girl, all knobby knees and elbows, could pass through too. Lupita placed the tray on a stand and stood, hands clasped together, motionless, listening and watching me. The little girl quickly began putting filled plates in front of each guest.

"I also took some aspirin out of an aspirin bottle stored in the kitchen last night, but they turned out not to be aspirin—as Helena and Margot can attest," I went on. I was aware Helena was staring at me. Margot had her eyes shut, as if she were concentrating or praying.

My words kept filtering out, while my disengaged brain observed it all. *If Donovan were here, he'd be climbing the walls by now,* I thought, still unable to shut up. When I got scared I talked—I couldn't help it. I'd talked the whole time my brother Hugo had been knocked off a jungle gym at school and had seemed to be bleeding to death while we were waiting for the ambulance.

"I think whoever put whatever I took in the aspirin bottle wasn't expecting me to take it but hoped my uncle would."

There was a collective intake of breath, then a surprised hum of low voices as the guests commented to each other about this.

"So I'm going to go in and get the bottle, and Donovan and I are going to have it analyzed this afternoon," I went on, undaunted. Where were these words coming from? And the bluff. For all I knew, it was fifty miles to the nearest drugstore. "I'm telling you this as a warning. If someone here thinks he can hurt my uncle, that person is going to have to deal with me first."

No one said a word. Nor did they pick up their forks or spoons and begin eating. They seemed mesmerized. For all I knew, they thought they got a floor show with breakfast, or they were genuinely concerned. I couldn't discount that.

"Judith," Helena said finally.

Knowing I didn't want anyone to distract me, her

least of all, I spun around and headed toward the kitchen.

"Excuse me, señorita. Excuse me." Lupita followed, plucking at my arm, finally drawing me to a complete stop once we were alone behind the swinging door. The kitchen smelled like a bakery—rich, delicious.

"That medicine bottle—the one in the cabinet," she said. "It's not there. I—I threw it out."

Now it was my turn to stare.

"I'm sorry. The bottle was broken. I thought the medicine would not be good anymore, so I put it in the garbage."

No excuses were going to detract me. Not anymore. I was like a bloodhound hot on the trail. "Where's the garbage?" I asked, fully prepared to search through it.

"Gone, señorita. I am so sorry. I come to work at four-thirty every morning. I bake the muffins, cut up the fruit, clean things, and at five-thirty Raymond— he's the head wrangler—comes and takes the sacks of garbage down to the incinerator, where he burns everything. I did not know you wanted the medicine." Her large brown eyes looked scared.

With effort I swallowed back a temper tantrum that felt as if it were brewing right under the surface of my skin. Remembering how the bottle had looked, I couldn't really blame Lupita. Mom might have done the same thing.

"It's okay." I put my hand out and patted her arm. Her tense face visibly relaxed. "By the way," I said, deliberately softening my voice, "I'm Judith Nelson, Jeremiah's niece."

"I know. I have been eagerly awaiting your arrival," she said. "I am Lupita Diego." We shook hands. Her grip was firm, her face friendly. She may have thrown the bottle away, but I had the feeling I could trust her. "I have been with your uncle for almost fifteen years," she said. "And my mother, bless her soul, worked here before me. The ranch is my second home. To have it sold. . . ." Her eyes filled with tears.

"Yes, it must be hard. And I hope you don't think I'm blaming you. I can see why you'd have thrown the bottle out."

"Do you really think that someone intended to harm Señor Sloane?"

"Yes, I do. You, probably more than anyone around here, must know, see things," I said on impulse. Casting a glance at the closed door, I lowered my voice. "What do you think? Do you think his accident was an accident?"

I expected a denial. I really wasn't prepared for the confirmation I saw immediately fly to her eyes or for the quick jerk of her head agreeing with me. "Oh, yes, señorita. Ever since the first of the accidents, I have been convinced that someone wants great harm to come to your uncle. I have tried to warn him. But he thinks it's just bad luck. He thinks it's just age creeping up. I know that is behind the selling of the ranch. People say it is because of Señora Sloane, but I don't believe that. He loves it here. He always said he would be buried in the shadow of Silver Dome. . . ."

I thought of the rugged, formidable mountain I'd seen this morning. The idea of spending forever in the ground near it was not my idea of comfort.

"To leave this place will cause his death. I can feel it. I think the accidents have drained his will to live. The accidents have made him think he's too old to run it."

"I know about the well and the ladder," I said.

"The well he blames on a wild animal bumping him. A wild animal." She shook her head.

"Have there been more"—I hesitated—"accidents?"

"Oh, yes. Every few years for the last ten years he has had an accident of some kind."

"Lupita!" Helena's powerful voice carried right through the door. We looked at each other, startled, wondering, I think, if we'd unintentionally raised our voices so that anyone could hear.

"I must serve breakfast," Lupita apologized. "The guests must not be kept waiting."

Accidents could happen. Disasters. But nothing could interfere with the guests' comfort, I thought bitterly. Then I remembered that this was, after all, a hotel of sorts and that the enjoyment of the guests had to come first if you wanted to stay in business. "Of course. I'm sorry I detained you."

She clasped my arm. "I am so glad you have come. So glad."

"I am too. And thank you for being so honest."

"I love your uncle," she said simply.

Just talking to Lupita had calmed me down. There was too much to risk by losing my head. Now that Donovan's suspicions had been confirmed by Lupita, I'd better be very careful. I wouldn't be able to help Uncle Jeremiah if something happened to me.

I could imagine what Donovan would do when I

told him how indiscreet I'd been. His frown would probably go right through his head and come out on the other side.

In retrospect I felt ashamed. I'd lost it for a moment. But it wouldn't happen again. I'd be calm and professional. Pushing through the swinging door, I glanced at the faces of the people at the two tables. Most of them had resumed talking. Only Helena looked at me expectantly.

"Sorry to cause such a disturbance," I murmured, taking my seat. "I think I overreacted."

"I can't believe anyone's trying to harm your uncle," Helena said.

"I'm sure you're right. Last night was upsetting and then, having someone shoot near me this morning. . . . But for all I know, the person was aiming at a cactus and didn't see me standing there."

"Foul things, guns," Dr. Morgansting exclaimed.

That started a heated discussion on the pros and cons of gun control and took the focus off me. I unfolded the red-and-white-checked napkin and laid it across my lap. Then I picked up my spoon and scooped up a small piece of cantaloupe. It was cold and sweet and exactly what everyone else was eating.

After breakfast, unlike me, all the guests seemed to have somewhere to go and something to do. About six of them headed toward the corral and a morning ride. Susie, wearing a large floppy hat and tennis togs, went off with Chuck, who was carrying a tin bucket filled with some of the oldest tennis balls I'd ever seen and two wooden rackets, one of which looked as if it were missing some strings. I hadn't realized the ranch had a tennis court.

I'd counted on spending time with Uncle Jeremiah. Now that was out. The next best thing would be to talk to Mom—to hear her calm, reassuring voice and to ask some questions. Not that she'd know the answers. She hadn't been here for years. But at least I could brainstorm with her.

The first trick was to find the office. Going outside, I walked around the encompassing porch until I saw an open door with a Welcome sign posted above it.

The interior was small and rustic, with knotty-pine walls and a high, circular counter. Behind the counter, just like in the late-night movies, were old-fashioned mail slots. From where I stood, I could see Donovan's name over one. Amazingly, Rudy had a box too. *That must just kill Donovan,* I thought. There wasn't any mail in them. No letters for Donovan from his mother . . . or Holly. I wondered if he had been telling the truth about Holly, and I decided he had.

Just as I was ready to think there wasn't a phone, I heard a low, grumpy voice and realized that I wasn't alone. Peering over the counter, I discovered Dr. Morgansting sitting in a low chair in front of a small desk on which rested a phone. He had the receiver glued to his ear, holding it in place with a massive hunched-up shoulder. He glanced at me, his eyes devoid of any interest. I turned and retreated to a worn armchair near the window and picked up a magazine from a rack.

Dr. Morgansting surfaced, holding the receiver to his chest. "Do you mind? This is a private conversation."

"Sorry," I murmured and exited through the screen door. At least there was a phone, and it was in working order. Waiting for Dr. Morgansting to finish, I sat for a moment on the porch in a slung-back canvas chair.

Mom and civilization were only a dial tone away, but even I had to admit that there was a rough beauty about this place. Gobs of purple, white, and pink petunias overflowed redwood boxes everywhere along the base of the porch. Beyond them was a small border of lawn where I'd seen the cottontails earlier. Beyond it was hard-packed sandy desert with clumps of cactus. The individual cottages sprang out from the main lodge like spokes from a wagon wheel.

A noise made me turn to see if Dr. Morgansting was coming out. Instead, I saw Margot reflected in the glass as she opened the window to her room. Seeing me, she pulled the curtain shut. Dr. Morgansting was certainly taking his time, I thought irritably.

Next, my attention shifted to a line of red ants carrying crumbs from the porch, down the two steps and into the grass. Somehow the ants made me think of transportation and cars—my Matilda in particular. I hoped Rudy would have her working soon. I didn't like the idea of being trapped here without my car, although there was a battered ranch station wagon and a pickup truck. I supposed I could use either of them if I needed to.

The air was pleasantly hot, but I couldn't relax enough to enjoy it. Guilty replays of the breakfast scene kept bombarding my mind. Why hadn't I kept my mouth shut? How would I ever explain what I'd done to Donovan? He'd be angry—and I couldn't blame him. I'd been immature—no, worse than that, *stupid!*

Giving up on the phone, anxious to get away from my own thoughts, I got up and went back inside the main lodge. It seemed homier than it had last night. The white walls wore hammered-tin light fixtures as large as mirrors, and each one had a candle-shaped light attached. Around the room brightly painted clay candlesticks sat on heavy carved-oak furniture. Large turquoise, red, and yellow paper flowers were skill-fully arranged in a pottery bowl on the coffee table in front of a curving white couch. The brown and yellow plaid couch in front of the walk-in fireplace, where Uncle Jeremiah had been last night, had the pillows all fluffed up. I wondered if Lupita had cleaned the room before cooking breakfast.

Bookshelves filled two of the walls, one of which had an arch to the entryway. The third window-filled wall faced the porch. And the baby grand stood in front of the fourth wall.

Walking over to the piano, I lifted the cover and put a finger on middle C, former childhood battles over piano lessons with Mom echoing through my mind. Stubbornly I'd refused to take them after a year. Hugo was the pianist of the family, I'd argued. I was the athlete. Fingering the keys lightly, I felt a moment of regret. The piano gleamed from having been well taken care of. The black had a rich, velvety feel; the cool ivory, while yellow with age, was in perfect con-dition. Instinctively I knew what Donovan must think of all the elephants slaughtered, and knew on some level I agreed with him. That made two things—except we'd never know what had been in that aspirin bottle now.

My anxiety returned with the force of a blow. Hearing footsteps, I whirled around and moved away from the piano like a guilty child. Helena appeared in the doorway, the scent of a rose perfume drifting in seconds after like a shadow. All business, she flicked a light switch, bathing the darkened room in brightness. She'd changed outfits again. Now she was wearing a deep-purple silk caftan. But what caught my eye was the tape recorder in her hand and the silver snake bracelet with turquoise eyes encircling her arm.

I expected her to say something about this morning and braced myself. Donovan might be leery of Rudy, but Helena was the one person I wasn't sure about. In spite of Donovan's assurance that her gun wasn't the one that had shot at us, I knew what I'd seen and how it had unnerved me.

"I'm going to play the piano and exercise my voice," she explained. "I do this every morning." She glided onto the bench, arranging her skirt, and placed the recorder carefully on the seat beside her. Then, kicking off her sandals, she pressed her bare feet onto the pedals while her lovely, long-fingered hands curved over the keyboard. She cocked her head, looking sideways up at me. Although she didn't actually say it, I felt the message. She wanted privacy. I was facing another dismissal.

"See you later," I said. Only as I crossed over the threshold did she strike the first note of a scale, her voice matching it—a perfect pitch.

Just as I entered the hallway, I thought I saw someone dart around the corner. I followed and looked around the corner. No one. I peered into the dining room. The little girl was setting the two tables for lunch.

"Did anyone come through here?" I asked.

She shook her head and put a fork on a napkin.

Once again I went out on the porch. The main lodge was constructed in such a way that the living room, dining room, and kitchen were in the center while the office and a bedroom—Margot's, I thought, remembering what she'd told me last night—were on one side, all opening up to the wide porch that encircled the whole building. Several other single bedrooms were on the other. One I noticed had a *Do Not Disturb* sign slung loosely over the knob. Uncle Jeremiah's room, no doubt. There was a tray outside on the porch with the remains of a grapefruit, a pot for tea, and untouched toast. Somehow it was reassuring to see that he'd taken some breakfast.

The sun was halfway up the sky. The sky itself was deep blue, ribboned with streaks of very white clouds. I hoped Rudy would show up by lunch. I needed to get off this place and do something to get rid of the excess energy I could feel building. In the meantime, time hung heavily on my hands. I didn't feel like reading or going back to my room. Maybe before Rudy came I should go back to Donovan's and clear my guilty conscience, tell him Lupita's suspicions matched our own.

Once again I followed the wash. It was longer than the way we'd come back to the ranch this morning, but at least I was sure of the way. Even so, I couldn't rid myself of the shivery feeling that someone was trailing after me, watching me. Several times I stopped and listened, but everything sounded all right. Flying insects whirred; birds continued chirping. A slight, very warm wind moved the brush, scratching one branch against another.

A hundred yards from his lean-to, I found Donovan stretching a piece of black plastic over a pit he'd dug.

"Hi," he said without looking higher than my tennis shoes. "I'll be right with you. I want to get this secured first."

"What is it?"

"I'm trying to condense moisture for drinking water. I read about how to do it, but so far it hasn't worked." He stretched the plastic taut and maneuvered a stick shaped like a needle that had a piece of rope tied around it. I could see all the muscles in his tanned arm working as he did what looked like an awkward sewing job. "I don't know why. Either I don't remember all the steps, or the guy who wrote it was lying."

"Or maybe it was a different time of the year," I suggested.

"That too. There!" Donovan crossed over and tugged at the other side, stretching the plastic tight.

"I have something unpleasant to tell you."

"What's that?" He still wasn't looking at me, but at what he was doing.

I told him how I'd behaved at breakfast. His reaction was pretty much as I'd expected—explosive.

"How could you do that? Especially when I asked you not to."

"I don't know. It just came out. I have a problem keeping secrets when I'm scared."

He opened his mouth as if to say something else, something undoubtedly scathing. I could see the huge struggle going on in his eyes—a struggle between saying what he really thought and what was polite. At last he mastered himself. "Spilt milk," he muttered. "Okay. No more about that. Did you find the aspirin bottle?"

"No."

He yanked at the plastic, which tore free and dropped limply in the hole. He groaned. "An hour's work wasted."

I wasn't sure if he meant the plastic ripping, the time spent thinking about the bottle, or maybe even our impromptu breakfast.

"Lupita saw the damaged bottle and threw it away," I told him. "Someone named Raymond burns the garbage every morning. So it's gone."

Donovan rocked back on his heels.

"I did uncover some information. Lupita agrees with you. She thinks someone's out to harm Uncle Jeremiah."

"Does she have any ideas who it might be?"

"I didn't get a chance to ask her. She was in the middle of serving breakfast. But I will later. In the meantime, I'm going to do some checking up on the guests—to see if I can uncover someone with a motive for revenge. Like Helena or Margot. I've been wondering why they hang around together. What do they possibly have in common?" I wanted to ask if he thought Margot had a crush on him, but I didn't.

"Friendships at guest ranches are often mysterious. People talk, become friends, and end up meeting each other here year after year. If they met somewhere else or saw each other all the time, they probably wouldn't be able to stand each other. The ranch is their only contact."

"Hmm. What about Dr. Morgansting?"

"A misanthrope. But I don't think it's a guest who wishes your uncle harm." He moved closer. I could smell the sunscreen he'd smeared across his nose. I could even have counted the scattering of little freckles on his high cheekbones.

"I think Rudy's the prime suspect."

"Yes, I know. Even my limited brain function understands that," I said.

"Be sure to ask him directly this afternoon or this evening, whenever you plan to see him. I'm sure he'll tell you."

I laughed. "Oh, you're wonderful! I admit one mistake, and you're going to hold it against me for days. I can tell you're an only child just from that," I said, my own anger flashing. "Well, you can rest assured that I won't blurt everything out to Rudy."

Instead of a snappy comeback, the edges of Donovan's lips twitched. *Why, he's teasing me,* I thought. The realization had an immediate effect. My annoyance dissolved into a muddle of feelings, mostly positive.

"I wonder if we should get someone to keep an eye on Jeremiah," Donovan said.

"I don't know." I thought for a moment. With his leg injury, Uncle Jeremiah did seem more vulnerable in one way and less in another. It wasn't as if he could go places and be a target. On the other hand, someone could— "Oh, my gosh!"

"What?"

"Helena told me Uncle Jeremiah had decided to rest in bed today. He's seeing no one, not even me. What if Uncle Jeremiah isn't all right? What if he's lying in his room drugged . . . or hurt?" A myriad of horrible fantasies swept through my mind.

"I think he's all right," Donovan said slowly. But I could see the doubt reflected.

"Wait a minute. Here I go, rushing to panicky conclusions again, saying whatever goes through my mind. I'm sure he's fine. I did see a breakfast tray outside his room," I added, trying to reassure us both.

But anxiety was building. My muscles were tightening; my smile felt artificial. I'd told myself I'd watch everything, and I'd done it again—completely fallen for the explanation Helena had given me. What I should have done. . . . Well, I could still do it. I'd go back and knock on Uncle Jeremiah's door. I'd see with my own eyes that he was okay and if there was anything I could do for him.

"I'm going back. I want to make sure he's in his room."

"If anything seems out of the ordinary, come and get me."

"Okay." Once again I could feel the unspoken attraction between us—as if there were a magnetic cloud stubbornly trying to pull us together. "See you later."

Once I was out of sight of Donovan's camp, I broke into a jog. *Please let Uncle Jeremiah be all right,* I prayed in time to the *thunk* of my feet on the hard-packed earth.

At first glance the ranch seemed deserted. The corral was empty. No one was on the porches soaking up the sun. A dry ache had settled in my throat. I wanted water—gallons of it, icy cold. But I didn't dare stop at the kitchen first. I sprinted up onto the porch of the main lodge. Then suddenly I was at the door to Uncle Jeremiah's room. The breakfast tray was gone. I raised my hand to knock . . . and stopped.

What if Helena was right and he was sleeping and I woke him? I thought of last night—how weak and frail he'd seemed. Maybe I was letting this morning's scare get to me. I walked a few feet down the hall where there was a window. The window was closed, and the interior hidden by a white, gauzy curtain. I pressed my nose against the glass, squinting. Then, feeling extremely self-conscious, I pulled back and made sure no one was coming.

Giving up, I went back to the door and raised my hand. If I woke him, too bad. I had to know everything was all right. I tapped lightly. No answer. Just as I was about to try the knob, I realized I could hear his voice. Gruff, shaky, with an edge of anger, he seemed to be chewing somebody out. I backed away. So, he was all right. My fears had been for nothing. Okay, I'd follow Helena's advice and leave him alone until he wished to be disturbed.

CHAPTER SIX

Immediately after lunch I cornered Lupita and asked her to keep her eye on Uncle Jeremiah.

"I know you're busy, and I'm certainly willing to pay you," I told her.

"Pay me for taking care of Señor Sloane? I wouldn't think of it."

"I didn't mean to insult you," I said, wishing I'd phrased it more sensitively.

"I know. You are young. You do not realize matters of the heart have no price tag." Her eyes softened. "Of course I will watch over Señor Sloane—as I always do, but even more so."

"Good. Thanks. You took him a tray this morning?"

"Yes, and at noon. Not chili like the guests, but a fruit salad. He is resting. I saw him." She pointed both forefingers at her own eyes.

The little girl came skipping through the kitchen. Lupita introduced me to her nine-year-old daughter, Conception.

"Three generations will have been at the ranch," I said.

"Yes. As I've said before, this is our second home."

From the kitchen I went to the office. I had a jolt when I discovered Dr. Morgansting using the phone again. A heavyset bleached-blond woman was behind the desk, reading a magazine. I introduced myself. Disinterested gray eyes flicked up at me. She said her name was Sophie and asked what I wanted in a manner that let me know it had better not require much effort on her part.

Hoping Dr. Morgansting was too wrapped up in his conversation to hear me, I asked her where the old guest registers of the ranch were. She glanced at a cupboard beneath the mailboxes and then up at me.

"I don't know if I'm supposed to give you that information," she replied. Her eyes were engaged in a battle between the print and dealing with me.

I fought back—successfully—an irritable response. "Since the ranch is due to close forever in several weeks, I can't see that it matters."

"It's not up to me to decide whether it does or doesn't," she replied. "I'm just not budging without the okay from Mr. Sloane."

"Thanks, anyway," I said, coldly sarcastic. But she'd turned her attention back to the magazine and didn't respond.

I went back to the cottage and changed again into jeans and a red-and-white-striped T-shirt just in case Rudy appeared. I knew from last night I wanted my legs to be covered up, just as I knew I didn't want my hair whipping into my eyes. I pulled it back into a ponytail, braided it, and caught that end in a rubber band as well. Not exactly gorgeous looking, but practical. I ended up rummaging through my suitcase and pulling out a small chiffon scarf and tying it into a bow over the rubber band. That looked less severe and added some color.

For all I knew, Rudy's invitation last night had been a momentary gesture of goodwill. Today perhaps he'd had second thoughts. Maybe fixing the water hose in Matilda hadn't been as simple as he'd thought, or maybe he'd gotten involved with something at his ATV park. I'd read for a while on the porch. If he showed up, fine. If he didn't, maybe I'd take a siesta.

Borrowing a mystery book from the bookshelf in the main lodge, I sat on the porch. Mrs. Jamison and Mrs. Bentley were on chaises in the shade, reading as well. Just as I was getting sleepy, Rudy came zipping up the gravel road to the ranch. He stopped abruptly in front of the porch, spattering gravel onto the grass. For some reason I'd been expecting him to drive up in Matilda. Disappointment over not seeing my car vied with relief at seeing him.

Rudy swung his leg over the ATV as if he were dismounting a horse and came sauntering up the flagstone walk. He wasn't wearing a shirt. His darkly tanned chest was powerful—a weight lifter's chest—his arms thick, strong.

He nodded to the two other women and grinned at me. "Hi, Judy. Are you okay?"

"Yes," I answered, puzzled. Asking me that was tantamount to admitting he'd taken the shot. Surely. . . .

"Why are you looking at me like that?" Rudy asked.

"How did you know? I mean, why wouldn't I be all right?"

"When I brought your suitcase last night, Donovan told me you'd been sick."

"Oh, *that*." Relief flooded me. I laughed nervously. "I ate something or had a mild flu. I was sick for a little while." I debated quizzing him about the aspirin and then decided against it. I'd promised Donovan to keep what we suspected to ourselves. If I told Rudy, he might draw some conclusions of his own.

"You look fine. Rested. What are you doing, reading?" He nodded his head to the book face down in my lap.

"Not really. It's too hot to concentrate. I've been waiting—for you."

His smile widened. "Now that's what a guy wants to hear." He flopped down into the chair next to mine.

"Where's my car?"

"Bad news, Judy. Two of the hoses are shot, and the fan belt is about to go. It'll be a few days."

"But you said— I need— *Rudy, I want my car!*"

"Then I'll make an effort to hurry things along." Rudy put his hand on my arm. "Don't get freaked."

"You're right. I don't know why I'm so uptight. I just feel so stranded without it, that's all."

"You are stranded." He grinned again. His teeth were large and white and straight. "There isn't anywhere to go except my place, and that's why I'm here —to take you."

"Even if there isn't anywhere to go, I like the idea of being able to get into my car and take off," I persisted.

"Take one of my ATVs— No, make that an

ATC—a four-wheeler. Something tells me you'll feel safer on one of those."

"I wouldn't know what to do with either one," I said, about to dismiss his offer. I reconsidered quickly, realizing that already I was feeling better.

"I'll show you. Come on, let's go. But first let me fill these. I meant to this morning and never got around to it." He went to his ATV and returned with a canteen. "First rule of the desert—never go off without plenty of water. Out here water can be the difference between life and death."

The kitchen was deserted. All the lunch dishes were done. Two pies sat on the counter, cooling. Overhead a fan whirled lazily. Rudy downed two soft drinks and filled the canteen. In spite of the normalcy of everything Rudy was doing, Donovan's persistent suggestion that he was behind whatever was going on had made an unwilling impression.

Once we were underway, the professional side of me had a continual battle with the daredevil. I'd seen the ward of brain- and spinal-damaged patients in our hospital at home too many times. Knowing how easy it would be to injure my head or break a bone if I fell off, I held tightly to Rudy as we bounced along the road.

"Look!" Rudy pointed to the steep foothill ahead of us.

What looked like ants were crawling out of clouds of dust and up the face of it. As we drew closer, I could see they were ATV riders.

"That's my place," Rudy said proudly.

"I saw you riding early this morning," I said, congratulating myself on how subtly I'd eased into interrogating him. Donovan would be proud of me.

"You couldn't have seen me." Rudy threw me a quick look over his shoulder. "I was working on your car. Must have been someone else."

Someone else. But who?

We lurched off the road and across the rough terrain. A couple of times Rudy used his booted foot to kick at a cactus that was in his way as we passed. The violent desecration bothered me, but I didn't say anything. There were so many cacti, a few wouldn't be missed, I thought. Still. . . .

We came to a whitewashed shed. RUDY'S RECREATIONAL PARK was scribbled in big letters on a makeshift sign. *All-day rides, $5.00. Ask about our seasonal specials*. Rudy cut the engine. My ears rang with silence. Dust gritted between my teeth; even my eyes felt ringed with dirt.

"Hey, Max!" Rudy shouted. "You in there?"

A dark, tousled head poked up from below the shelf, followed by narrow shoulders and long torso.

"This is Judy," Rudy said. "Judy, my kid brother, Max."

We said hello to each other.

Max looked a lot like Rudy except that he was about a foot taller and had the lanky body and troubled complexion of a teenager. Rudy asked Max how many people had checked through. Max told him there'd been three ATVs, two ATCs, and a couple of dirt bikes.

Rudy frowned. "I told you not to let dirt bikes in. We're not set up for them yet."

"No big deal. I sent them up the trail to Silver Dome. Told them to watch for the orange ribbons."

"Insurance, Max. How many times do I have to tell you?"

"What's the difference between dirt bikes and ATVs?" I asked.

"ATVs use wide trails, low hills. Dirt bikes use narrow trails, and the riders like to do crazy things— like jumping or going straight up a high hill."

"Riders like Rudy," Max filled in. He had Rudy's infectious grin and a chipped front tooth.

"Yeah, but *I* know what I'm doing, and if I break my neck, I'm not going to sue me out of business!" Rudy turned to me, hands on his hips, his biceps golden in the sun. "Once I get Jeremiah's land, then I'll turn that into ATV territory and use the foothills for dirt bikes." He smiled. "I'm hoping if you have a good time today, maybe you'll convince him."

There was a roar from behind us. A guy wearing a tattered sleeveless shirt, jeans, and boots that looked as if they were made for stomping drove up. I couldn't keep my eyes off a spiderweb, complete with spider in the center of it, that he had tattooed on his arm. He asked some questions and finally bought an entry into the park.

"I thought I'd let Judy use the ATC," Rudy said to Max.

Max drew his dark brows together. "You can't. I rented it already."

"How about Little Red?"

"I'll get it." Max left the stand and walked to a metal shed about six hundred yards away.

"You get that broken lock fixed yet?" Rudy called out.

"No . . . later." Max disappeared inside the shed and reappeared rolling what looked like a child's bright-red version of an ATV, not nearly as threatening as the monster Rudy was on.

"Listen, Rudy, I'd feel more comfortable wearing a helmet. Are there any?"

"A couple." Max went into the shed and rummaged around.

"I know what you're thinking," Rudy said. "A shoestring operation. But it won't be for long. Pretty soon I'm going to have the biggest ATV park around —bigger than the ones outside Yuma or the Mojave."

Max thumped several helmets on the broad shelf in front of us. Rudy leaned over. He discarded one and handed me the other.

"Try this. It may be a little big, but it'll do the job."

Even though it felt too heavy, I kept it on.

Rudy showed me how to kick-start. The smaller engine sounded like a wasp trapped inside a window. Next he showed me how to shift gears, where the throttle was, how to stop. Like motorcycles, ATVs didn't have a reverse gear, he explained. He showed me how to maneuver it around if I wanted to change direction.

At first we rode up and down the road leading to Rudy's park. Next we tackled a hill. As I was going up, a tire hit a rock and spun crazily to one side and nearly tipped over.

Okay, that's enough of this, I thought, coming to a stop. My jaw hurt from clenching my teeth; my arms ached from the vibrations of the handles; my thigh muscles were trembling from the exertion of constantly bracing myself.

"Are you okay?" Rudy was beside me.

"I think so, but it scared me."

"Maybe I'm pushing you too hard. Let's stick to flat ground until you feel safe. We'll tackle hills later."

I liked how Rudy instinctively knew how to treat sticky issues. Had Donovan been here, he would have insulted me in some way so that I'd have risen to the challenge and probably broken my neck in the process. As it was, I meekly followed Rudy's oversized three-wheeler on my small one, content to let him lead the way.

But even riding on the flat desert wasn't as easy as he'd implied, and certainly not as easy as the dirt road had been. There were cacti to dodge, fissures to avoid . . . but as he'd predicted, riding on my own was more fun than being on the back of his.

A couple of hours later, when I'd had enough sun and stress and was anxious to get back to a gallon of water and some shade, once again Rudy insisted I keep the ATV for my stay.

Relief at having wheels under me was dimmed only slightly by the reaction I knew Donovan would have if he discovered I'd joined the enemy.

"I think I'd just as soon no one knew I had this—at least right now," I said.

"Why?" Rudy looked genuinely perplexed. "Your uncle won't care—if that's what you're worried about. In fact, I'd like him to know."

"I hope you aren't being nice to me just to influence Uncle Jeremiah." Rudy started to object, but I waved him silent. "Because I don't know if I can support your cause. I have some reservations about ATVs."

"Fair enough. I don't want you to endorse something you're not a hundred percent behind. No, that's being too generous. I hope even if you're only fifty percent behind me, you'll give my place the benefit of a doubt and ask Jerry to sell to me." He eyed me levelly. "Anybody else who's bidding can say whatever they want, but *you* aren't going to find out what they're really going to do with the land. You do know that, don't you?"

Actually, that hadn't occurred to me. "I suppose you're right."

"At least I'm up front. Now Donovan—who knows what goes on in his head?"

I was confused. "Donovan hasn't bid on the land, has he?" Somehow this morning I'd gotten the feeling that he'd like to bid on the land but hadn't. I tried to think back to the exact wording and couldn't.

"Somebody's bidding against me. I think it's him. I'm sure that's what's behind his back-to-nature ecology bit. It's a cover."

"Kind of a dramatic cover. I don't think anybody would go to all that trouble. Besides, why would he? What's the point?"

"By playing poor, by promising to save the desert, he hopes to con Jerry into selling at a low bid. Then he'll turn right around and resell it and make a profit." Rudy said all this with such conviction it was hard to just dismiss it.

I didn't dare say anything. I was afraid I'd just start babbling, expressing my fear, my confusion, one more time today. "I'd better be getting back," I said finally.

"Sure. Whatever you want." To my relief Rudy let the matter drop. Good-naturedly he escorted me back to the ranch and suggested parking the ATV behind my cottage, where it wasn't visible from the road. After I got off, Rudy took a chain with a lock from his ATV and looped it around the frame of mine and then around a peppertree. "I don't think anyone would steal this, but you can't be too sure."

"Oh, coyotes can't open doors, but they can ride ATVs?"

He glanced at me quickly. "Humans ride ATVs, and we've had some trouble with people swiping ours."

Maybe that explained this morning. "Did someone take one this morning?"

Rudy shrugged. "Max didn't say anything. Why? Oh, you're thinking back to the one you saw this morning?"

"Yeah."

"Why is it I get the feeling something weird happened and you're not leveling with me? So you saw an ATV early this morning." He was studying me, his eyes unreadable, his expression serious. "What's the deal? What happened?"

"Nothing, Rudy."

"I can see from your face that it wasn't *nothing*. If Donovan or anybody has told you something about *my* ATVs, I'd like to hear it. I'd like to be given a chance to defend my place, my recreational vehicles. I really want to make a go of this, Judy. It means a lot to me. It's my life."

"A scary thing happened. I was visiting Donovan in

his camp. Someone took a shot at us. A few minutes later we saw an ATV headed in this direction."

"And Donovan naturally assumed it was me."

I bit my lip to keep from admitting that was true. "We talked it over and decided we couldn't make a snap judgment. But, Rudy, he'll be very angry if he knows I've told you."

"Don't worry. I won't tell him." Rudy's wide brow was furrowed; then it smoothed. "It wasn't me. I don't own a gun. Even if I did, I wouldn't shoot it—especially at you."

"I believe you."

He jammed his hands into his pockets and kicked at a small stone, sending it arcing into the air a few feet away. "Just one darn thing after another," he muttered. "I'll talk to Max. I'll get back to you on this one."

"Okay." I could only hope I'd made the right decision in telling Rudy. Donovan would think I'd lost my mind again. On the other hand, maybe with the three of us working independently, we'd outwit whoever was behind whatever scheme was going on. *Right,* I thought. *Rationalize the fact you've blurted out everything.* Not quite everything. I hadn't told Rudy about the aspirin.

I sighed. It was good I hadn't chosen detective work. Even as a little girl I hadn't been good at doing puzzles. I didn't have the patience.

Saying maybe he'd stop by that evening, Rudy took off with a revved-up roar and a splash of gravel.

Once I was in my room, not bothering with a glass, I drank straight from the faucet in huge, satisfying gulps. Then I took another shower. As I was toweling my hair dry in the bathroom, I thought I heard the screen door to my room open and footsteps on the tile floor.

"Who's there?" I called out.

No one answered.

Had Rudy come back to tell me something? Surely he wouldn't just walk in. Wrapping a towel securely around me, I peered into the room.

No one was there. But I knew I'd heard something, someone. I crept to the window and peered out. On one of the pathways about a hundred yards away, Chuck and Susie were locked in an embrace. A maid wheeling a cart filled with clean towels was disappearing around a corner. I let the curtain fall.

I locked my door. Maybe coyotes didn't open doors, but until some issues had been resolved, I was going to keep mine locked—at least, while I was inside. Then I finished drying my hair.

As I reached into my suitcase for my clothes, my fingers brushed against something unexpectedly soft —furry. I screamed. Yanking my hand out, I threw back the top of the suitcase. There, on top of my green shirt, was a small, very dead furry creature.

Not allowing myself to think, I went back to the bathroom. I grabbed a towel I'd used to soak up water on the floor. I gingerly picked up what I now realized was a cottontail that had lost a battle with a car—or an ATV—some time ago, judging by its condition.

For a fleeting, irrational second I wondered if Rudy had sneaked back and stuck it into my suitcase. Some wary part of my mind had noticed that he'd been near at least two of the times something awful happened. And even with the gunshot, we had seen an ATV. Was he pretending to like me merely to catch me off guard and then terrorize me? If so, it was working, I thought dryly.

Holding my breath, I unlocked the door, pushed open the screen, and dropped the cottontail outside on the porch. Next, I excised my green shirt with two fingers, tossing it onto the floor of my closet. A piece of paper fluttered like a white butterfly to the floor. But my attention was still focused on the grossness of what I'd uncovered. There was no way I'd wear the shirt until I washed it, and even then. . . . I shuddered. Who would do such a thing? Why?

A massive surge of anxiety flashed through me. To fight it off, I busied myself emptying my suitcase, rapidly sticking shirts, pants, skirts, blouses, underwear, shoes into the closet and the empty dresser. Then I closed the suitcase and stuck it out of sight behind the door. It was only then, as I was glancing around the room, that my eyes lighted on the piece of paper. I hesitated, already knowing somehow it had a message. I picked it up and unfolded it.

GO AWAY! it said in neat, square block letters—the kind a child in kindergarten might make.

"I've got news for you, whoever you are," I said out loud. "I'm a lot bigger than a cottontail. I won't be such an easy target."

Brave words. Out here in unfamiliar country I *was* an easy target. Hadn't I been shown that twice already?

I quickly dressed in clean jeans and a light cotton blouse, anxious to get to the lodge where there should be more people, where I'd be completely safe.

As I came up onto the porch, I heard voices coming from the dining-room area. I tiptoed closer.

"I want to know what's going on," a voice I recognized as Helena's said. "If you won't tell me . . . Judith. . . ."

My skin prickled at the sound of my name. I edged closer.

"Shh!" another voice admonished.

"Judith!"

I jumped. Blood shot into my face. Guiltily I turned and faced Uncle Jeremiah. He was sitting in the corner of the porch in his wheelchair. A light knitted cotton blanket covered his lap and legs. A nearby chair held a supply of magazines and a glass of water.

"Uncle Jeremiah! What a surprise! How are you? I hoped to see you this morning, but Helena said you didn't want to be disturbed." The torrent of nervous words burst forth like a dam breaking. I sank into the chair near him. What must he have thought of me, creeping around, eavesdropping, and now babbling like an idiot?

"I have my good moments . . . and my bad. My breathing hasn't been so hot lately, but I expect it will improve again." Uncle Jeremiah extended his bony, blue-veined hand and covered my hot, nervous one. In spite of the heat of the afternoon, his hand was cool.

"Listen, Uncle Jeremiah," I said, keeping my voice low. "You know what medications you're supposed to take, don't you?"

He looked surprised. "For my breathing? Of course. A little bump on the head hasn't made me senile."

How could I phrase what I needed to say so that he wouldn't know about last night and get alarmed? When I couldn't think of a way, I did my usual trick —blurted out the truth. "I'm scared to death it was meant for you. Donovan and Lupita say you've had some close calls."

"Phhft," he scoffed. "There've been a couple of accidents. You know, accepting the fact that accidents happen in this world is hard for anyone. Everyone wants to blame somebody, something. The only time I felt threatened was two years ago with the well incident. The cover had been removed. I was hit from behind. At the time I thought it might be a person— someone out to rob a guest at the ranch. But in retrospect it could have been an animal bumping me behind the knees."

One of those infamous coyotes, I thought.

"How about the fall from the ladder? Was that an accident?"

"I can't swear to it." His gaze didn't meet mine, and it seemed to me I could see his jaw muscle twitch, as if he were holding it tight. And I got the distinct impression that he was having second thoughts.

"I know what happened to me wasn't an accident," I said when he didn't elaborate further. "It was deliberate. So until I get to the bottom of what happened, I don't want you to take anything without really examining it. If you take an aspirin, make sure that's what it is."

"I will. But you be careful. I don't want you looking into anything. I want you totally uninvolved. If anything happened—"

"I'm not going to put myself at risk," I interrupted,

trying to reassure him. "I'm talking about a little snooping, nothing major. Like I'd like to look at some of the old guest books—or records of guest registrations for the last ten years. May I do that?"

"Sure. Why? What are you thinking?" A perky light had come into his pale eyes. He was sitting a little straighter in his chair.

"I can't put it into words yet," I said. "But I think there may be a connection between things that have happened to you—the so-called *accidents* and when certain guests have been here. I want to check it out. But I also don't want anybody to know what I'm doing. Unfortunately, Sophie won't let me take the ledgers without your permission."

"You've got it."

But already I was having second thoughts about Sophie or anyone knowing that I had the books. A careless word from her to someone would result in more than a dead cottontail. I heard myself telling Uncle Jeremiah that I just wanted to get the ledgers without anyone knowing.

"Sophie goes off duty at five. A wrangler, Oscar, takes over from then until nine. He won't care. Help yourself. They're in the cupboard behind the desk."

"Okay. Thanks. Now, I want you to tell me about your *accidents*. When they happened and what happened. I want to know everything you remember, no matter how insignificant it seems."

CHAPTER SEVEN

It turned out there had been four incidents over the last seven years. Not counting the fire, Uncle Jeremiah told me.

"The fire? What fire?"

Uncle Jeremiah dismissed it as if it were nothing. It was totally unrelated and had been deliberate. A wrangler, angry over being fired, had dumped things around in the office, then set a wastebasket on fire. Fortunately it had been discovered before any major damage had been done.

However, in 1981, April or May, he'd been leading a horseback ride. They'd stopped for lunch halfway up Silver Dome at a deserted old mining town, Vilagos. On the ride back, when the group had broken into a fast lope, his saddle had suddenly come loose. He'd fallen underneath the horse and had barely escaped being trampled to death—as it was, he'd suffered two broken ribs and a fractured arm. Later a wrangler swore the cinch looked as if it had been slashed.

The next accident had happened in 1983. He remembered that because Aunt Anna had been very ill. Preoccupied with her, he hadn't spent much time with the guests that season. Somehow he'd eaten something that had nearly killed him. Food poisoning, he'd thought, although no one else had gotten sick. He'd ended up being transported to the hospital in Tucson, where he'd stayed two weeks.

"When? What time of year?" I asked.

Early May, he thought.

So both of those had happened right near the end of the guest season. I was tempted to ask if any of the current guests had been present. But with effort I curbed my tongue and let him continue uninterrupted. I didn't want him to lose his train of thought.

Then there was the night excursion where he'd been lured into the desert and nearly knocked into the abandoned well.

"Donovan told me about that."

"Do you like Donovan?"

The question caught me by surprise. "Well, yes, I do." I looked down at my hands, feeling a telltale warmth slip up my neck and into my cheeks.

"When did the well incident happen?" I asked.

"February '85."

So they'd been about two years apart. That was something to think about.

"It was about that time I leased the land to Rudy. Rudy's related to Lupita—third or fourth cousin. But there were some scruffy-looking characters who hung around him. I thought one of them had seen a diamond flashing on Mrs. Bentley's hand or knew how famous some of my guests were and decided it might be more profitable than scratching a living out of the desert."

"But you changed your mind?"

"Not exactly. As I say, I didn't suspect Rudy. But I explained the situation to him. We decided no one but him or Max—Max is his brother—should use any of the ranch facilities."

"I've met Max. And by the way, Rudy would like me to put in a good word for him. He wants this ranch."

"I know. But I'm having second thoughts." His gaze drifted away. "I love it here. My memories, my life are in everything as far as you can see. I know every niche of Silver Dome. There's a ghost town halfway up. An old abandoned silver mine as well. Heck, everywhere you turn around up there, there's history." His air supply dwindled into a wheezing cough. "As for the ranch, your Aunt Anna and I planted that strip of grass," he continued. "I helped build every single cottage, you know. *I am* the ranch, in a way."

My throat tightened. "Then maybe you should stay."

"But the reality is I'm old—too old to run the place by myself. I should take the money and retire some-where, where the living is easy."

"Mom hopes you'll come to us."

"Easy life, I said. That means no snow, no freezing winds. I'm thinking of Tucson, maybe Florida. These old bones want heat."

"Are you considering Rudy's offer?"

Uncle Jeremiah shot me a keen sideways glance. "Yes, *but*—and it's the *but* that bothers me. All the noise, the damage. If you could have seen this country when I first came here. . . . The silent, haunting beauty of Silver Dome. Now, motorcycles, those fat-tired things Rudy rides, are creeping up it. No respect for tradition, the past. I just don't know. I can't decide."

"Who else is bidding?"

There was a pained expression on Uncle Jeremiah's face. He rubbed the knuckles of one knobby hand with the other and sighed. "No one."

"No one? But I thought you had three interested buyers."

He shook his head. "I told Rudy that to keep him from pestering me to death. So don't you tell him anything different."

"I won't. Scout's honor."

"Truth is, the place is a white elephant. Too far away to lure large numbers of people, not enough modern conveniences for many. I always wanted it small, private."

Lupita and Conception appeared, bringing a pitcher of lemonade and a tray holding two tall glasses filled with ice cubes. Lupita told Uncle Jeremiah that the refrigerated-food truck would arrive that afternoon. While they discussed business, I sipped my lemonade and watched Conception as she hopped up and down the two low, flat steps, first on one foot and then the other. The day's events were catching up with me; I was exhausted.

After they left I could see Uncle Jeremiah was tired too. "I think we both need a nap," I said. I asked if I could wheel him to his room, but he said he was just fine there. I wanted to get the guest books just as soon as Sophie went off duty, so I opted for the living room rather than my room.

Relieved to see the living room was empty, I chose the longest couch, the one where Uncle Jeremiah had been last night, kicked off my shoes, and lay down. With Uncle Jeremiah doing sentry duty on the porch and other people around, I was perfectly safe. Within seconds I was asleep.

The clang of the dinner bell woke me. Disoriented, aware of voices in the background, I discovered a number of the guests sitting on the far side of the room—not wanting to disturb me, I guess—having drinks before dinner. So stiff I could hardly walk, I murmured hello in passing. They were dressed for dinner, I noticed. The men wore light jackets or sweaters; the women were in dresses or fancy evening pants.

Outside it had cooled down. The sky was ablaze with colors. I stopped, overcome by the violent, passionate beauty of the shocking-pink sky. The setting sun had highlighted the puffs of clouds, making them seem edged with a gold filigree.

"If I could make a dress with those colors, I could sell it for a fortune," Margot said as she approached me. It was the first pleasant thing she'd said to me. In the fading light she had a slender beauty, dressed as she was in a white full-skirted dress, pulled in at her narrow waist by an apricot silk scarf. Her face seemed more relaxed. Maybe what I'd mistaken before for aloofness or jealousy was actually shyness.

"The scarf you're wearing almost matches it," I said. "You look lovely."

"Thank you." She took another step as if to pass me

and stopped. "Are you all right? You look like you got too much sun today. Your face is burned."

I touched my cheeks. My skin did feel hot.

"As fair as you are, you should watch out for sunstroke."

"I guess you're right. Thanks. I'll put more sunscreen on."

I waited until she was safely in the living room before I went into the office. Sophie was gone. A black-haired Mexican man was busily typing. I introduced myself and said I needed to get something out of the cupboard. He said to help myself, and as I searched through, I could hear the typewriter keys clicking away. I took four ledgers that were really similar to school composition books. Most carried three years of guests' signatures and occasionally comments about the ranch, the service, or a personal note to Uncle Jeremiah and/or his wife. I grabbed four of the most recent.

I paused at the front desk. "May I have a key to Room 3?"

He looked surprised. "A key? Guests don't usually lock their doors," he said. But he got up and pulled a key from out of the mailbox for Room 3 and handed it to me.

I thanked him, and with the books safely tucked against my chest, I hurried back to my room, eager to study them, and yet knowing I wouldn't be able to until later. There were only ten minutes, if that, until the next dinner bell. I didn't want to be late to two meals my first day.

I hid the guest books in my closet beneath my suitcase. Then I must have set a world record for dressing. I threw on a wine-colored paisley blouse and full cotton skirt. I pulled on panty hose and shoved my aching feet into high heels, determined to look properly dressed if it killed me.

The cottontail carcass was still by my front door. I shuddered. I hoped some cleanup detail would come along and remove it.

In the dining room Uncle Jeremiah was at the head of one table, sitting in what looked like a carved bishop's chair. There were two brightly colored pillows supporting his back. As I chose an empty seat between Susie and Dr. Morgansting, Donovan appeared in the doorway. He was neatly dressed in a yellow knitted golf shirt and khaki slacks and loafers. His hair was damp and curling from a recent shower. So much for roughing it in the desert. I smiled to myself, glad to see him.

He went directly to Uncle Jeremiah, leaned down to say something, and patted his shoulder. He was charming to everybody. He nodded to Helena and Margot, then spoke to someone else whose name I didn't remember—I thought she was Mrs. Jamison's daughter-in-law. He waved to someone else. He appeared to be the darling of the ranch. He finally worked his way over to me, pausing behind Dr. Morgansting.

"Excuse me, Dr. Morgansting. Would you mind switching seats? There's one at the table over there."

"Mind!" Dr. Morgansting exclaimed. "Yes, I'd mind. I like it right here."

Across the table Mrs. Jamison stood up. "Take mine, Donovan dear."

"I couldn't do that, Mrs. Jamison."

"Nonsense. I insist."

"In that case, thank you."

She glared at Dr. Morgansting. "Weren't you ever young? Ever in love?"

"No to both questions." Dr. Morgansting glared at her.

"We're not in love," I said hastily. "We barely know each other."

"Oh, you will be. I can feel it," Mrs. Jamison said and smiled.

Cupping her elbow, Donovan escorted her over to the other table. "That's occurred to me too," I heard him say in a low voice.

Dinner was stuffed pork chops. There was a broccoli soufflé and a salad of sliced oranges and red onion rings. The conversation focused on tomorrow's activity, which was to be a breakfast ride. Then Dr. Morgansting sourly observed that the stock market had gone down—again—and that he might leave a few days early.

I realized with a shock I had no idea *what* had been happening in the outside world, I'd been so intensely involved in the ranch and the dangers I'd experienced so far. Somehow here in the midst of people wearing jewels and fancy clothes, eating off china, using polished silver, it was hard to take the threats seriously. It was as if there were two separate worlds or I were taking part in a movie. . . .

"You're looking awfully thoughtful," Donovan said. There was what looked like a tender expression on his face.

"I was thinking about a dead cottontail I saw today." I hadn't planned to introduce the subject, but suddenly I was pleased with the idea and I proceeded, not saying where I'd found it, but trying to lure the person who had placed it in my suitcase to reveal something. "It had been killed by something . . . somebody."

"The little murders—the worst aspect of the desert," Helena said. Holding her knife and fork European fashion, she cut into her pork chop and took a neat bite.

"I used to cry when I was a girl when I'd see the ears, the bits of fur, the hind legs of the rabbits that had come to feed on the grass and fallen prey to the coyotes." Margot's voice dropped. "Sometimes at night you can hear them being killed. They scream— like women being tortured."

Gooseflesh traveled up my arms to the back of my neck.

"I remember how you used to cry over them when you were a little girl, Margot," Uncle Jeremiah said. His face was soft, tender. "I used to make the rounds before daybreak, trying to remove all traces of anything that had been killed during the night, so you wouldn't see."

"I didn't know that." Margot blushed and looked down at her plate. "That was very kind."

"You were such a timid little girl. Those long braids, those big eyes." He smiled at her.

Mrs. Jamison and Mrs. Bentley told some stories of adventures they'd had with coyotes and rabbits and even a mountain lion. Then Uncle Jeremiah told of local legends—a woman bandit who'd been hanged in the cottonwoods sixty years ago. I didn't pick up any information, but I had warned whoever had

planted the cottontail that I wasn't going to be si-
lenced or scared. At least I hoped I had.

For dessert we had the pies I'd seen earlier. "I feel
as if I just ate lunch, now dinner. By the time I leave I
may have to be rolled to my car."

"Lupita is a wonderful cook," Helena agreed. "I
wish I could lure her to L.A. after the ranch closes.
But all her family is here. She won't leave, she says."

We moved to the living room for coffee. While
we'd been at dinner, someone had built a roaring fire.
Donovan helped Uncle Jeremiah to the couch and
went to a cupboard, bringing out a worn backgammon
set and two dice cups. Chuck pulled out a jigsaw puz-
zle, and he and Susie spilled the contents onto a card
table. Another group took the Scrabble board. Still
another got some cards.

Uncle Jeremiah's cheeks had spots of color in them.
He obviously was eager to play the game. "What's the
score?" he asked. "How far ahead am I?"

Donovan opened the board and pulled out a yel-
lowing piece of paper that had numbers scribbled all
over it. "I'm afraid I'm in the lead."

Uncle Jeremiah's chin jutted out—my expression,
the one Rudy had commented on. I recognized it immediately. Smiling, I sank down across from them on
the Navaho rug.

"Not for long, you're not," Uncle Jeremiah said.
"Hurry up. Shake. We'll see who's first."

I was touched to see how Donovan dealt with Uncle
Jeremiah. He sort of played both sides, but so de-
viously and with such humor that I don't think Uncle
Jeremiah realized that he was being helped.

Helena pulled up a low-slung chair and sat beside

me. She had on a scoop-necked deep-red blouse with a matching red skirt. There were what looked like a dozen gold chains around her neck. She'd applied gold-flecked eye shadow and looked as if she were about to go on stage for *Aida*.

Margot drifted in—a vision in white—and stood beside her. "Shall we play some bridge?"

"Not tonight." Helena tilted her head back against the chair, her eyes closed.

"Head again?" Margot asked.

"Yes." Helena pressed both hands to her temples. "Just pounding. I think I'll go to my cottage."

"I'll walk with you."

"No! I want to go alone."

"Whatever you want." Soft as a moth Margot glided away from us. I remembered the angry voices earlier today. Had Margot been the person Helena had been arguing with? There was a quiet anger about Helena, an obsequiousness about Margot. Helena seemed so edgy. Was she reacting to my bringing up the cottontail? Did she know something? The memory of her carrying her gun flashed back. . . .

Without saying good night to anyone, which in itself was unlike her, Helena got to her feet abruptly and left the room. Only the scent of the rose perfume lingered, a teasing reminder. Getting to my feet, I took her chair and watched Uncle Jeremiah and Donovan for a while.

Margot sat on the window seat, a glass of sherry in her hand, staring out into the dark. What was she thinking, I wondered.

"Judith," Susie called out, "tomorrow is the breakfast ride to the ghost town, Vilagos. Are you going?"

"I don't think so. I don't ride."

"You have to come. It's your only chance to see it. And it's the last ride up there this season."

"Or ever," Mrs. Jamison said regretfully. "Oh, Jeremiah! I hate the thought of the ranch closing."

Several of the guests agreed.

Uncle Jeremiah scowled at the backgammon board and didn't answer.

"Can I walk there?" I asked. I had a vision of myself arriving at the ghost town on the ATV . . . of Donovan's furious face.

"It's a long walk, dear," Mrs. Bentley said. "I'm sure the wranglers can find you a nice, gentle horse that will plod along the way it's supposed to."

"I don't know. . . ."

"Donovan, you'll ride with her, won't you?" Uncle Jeremiah asked.

"Sure." Donovan looked over at me; his eyes, reflecting the firelight, seemed to have the bottomless depth of a lake. His hair had dried into rough curls. While he was gazing at me, Uncle Jeremiah took the opportunity to remove two of his men.

Oscar stuck his head in the doorway. "There's a phone call for Judith Nelson," he announced.

I jumped to my feet. "Mom—I completely forgot to call her. She must be wondering what has happened to me."

"I haven't talked to Virginia in ages," Uncle Jeremiah said. "Help me into my wheelchair, will you, Donovan?"

"I'll run on ahead," I said, "so she doesn't hang up." As I started across the room, I noticed the window seat was empty.

The office was deserted. The receiver had been put on the counter. I grabbed it up. "Hi, Mom, I'm sorry. I meant to call you," I blurted out.

"Mom?" Rudy's voice spilled into my ear. "No, it's me, Rudy."

"Oh, gosh, Rudy, I forgot all about you. . . ."

"This afternoon you were waiting for me; tonight I'm a forgotten man. You sure move fast."

"I'm sorry. I didn't mean it like that. Did you uncover anything?"

"Not much. It was Max you saw. But I know for sure he didn't shoot at you. He knows even less about guns than I do."

So the two events were unrelated. Good.

"Now about your car," Rudy continued. "They sent the wrong fan belt. It'll be another day at least."

There was a thump behind me as Donovan pushed the wheelchair over the metal door strip. Asking Rudy to wait a moment, I put my hand over the mouthpiece. "It isn't Mom, after all, Uncle Jeremiah." I couldn't look Donovan in the face.

"Who in the world is it, then?" Donovan asked.

"Rudy," I said meekly.

"Rudy? Why is *he* calling *you?*" Donovan challenged.

"He'd said maybe he'd come over tonight. It turns out he can't," I answered. "Not that it's any of your business."

"You're right. It isn't. Excuse me. Go right ahead."

But he continued standing there.

"I'll just finish with Rudy, Uncle Jeremiah. Then I'll call Mom. I know she'd love to talk to you."

I turned my attention back to the phone. "Sorry,

there's a bit of a commotion here," I explained to
Rudy. I could feel Donovan's eyes burning a hole in
my back.

"I'm sorry the garage fouled up. I know how much
having your car means to you. But you're not
stranded. Remember that."

"I will." I could tell Rudy wanted to chat, but I felt
really uncomfortable with Donovan and Uncle Jeremiah hovering.

"How about another early-morning ATV ride?" he
asked.

"I can't. I've agreed to go on the breakfast ride."

"I'm going into Tucson to get some supplies I need.
You could come too."

It was tempting. "Thanks, but I think I'll stick
around here." So we left when we'd meet again open-
ended.

"I'll try Mom," I said. I dialed home. The phone
rang and rang. I hung up. "She isn't home. I'm
sorry."

"Isn't home? Why isn't she? It's after eleven back
there," Uncle Jeremiah commented.

I laughed. "Mom has a dozen different causes.
She's out a lot."

"I'll bet if I gave in and went back with you, *I'd*
become one of those causes. She wouldn't be happy
until she had me all duded up, citified."

"Nobody could do that," Donovan said. "Besides,
you should stay here. This is where you belong." He
shot me a fierce glance. "Come on, let's finish our
game."

"Judith?" Uncle Jeremiah called out. "Are you
coming?"

"No, I think I'll turn in." Not exactly the truth. I wanted to start on the books, and if I waited much longer, I'd be too sleepy.

Going over to Uncle Jeremiah, I kissed him good night, then said good night to Donovan. As I watched their retreating backs, once again I found myself questioning Mom's decision that Uncle Jeremiah should come to us. Maybe taking Uncle Jeremiah away from here would drain the last bit of life from him. A terrible unsureness of what was the right thing to do settled around me like a shroud.

CHAPTER EIGHT

O nce I was in my room, I locked the door and pulled the curtains. Then I did a quick search, letting my breath out in a relieved sigh when I didn't turn up any scary objects. It took me all of five minutes to get ready for bed. I pulled on my yellow terry-cloth bathrobe over my cotton nightshirt, grabbed several sheets of paper from the desk drawer. Sitting cross-legged on the center of the bed, I spread the ledgers out in a fan. I started with April of 1981.

My heartbeat picked up when I realized that the thick scribbled writing was Helena Knight's signature. There was another name that didn't ring a bell, and then Margot Hill printed in tiny, neat letters. Farther down the page Elliot Morgansting had scrawled his name in a giant slant taking up two lines.

A tap on my door made me drop my pencil. "Just a moment," I called out. Flustered, I slid the books under my covers. "Who is it?" I asked before unlocking the door.

"It's Priscilla Bentley."

Mrs. Bentley? What did she want? I opened the door.

"Oh, you're ready for bed," she observed. "I'm sorry to disturb you. I saw your light. . . ."

"It's all right. I wasn't asleep. Come in," I said, holding the screen open.

"I won't keep you. I wanted to talk to you privately. I'd hoped to catch you when you came back from the phone call." She seemed out of breath, nervous.

I almost said, "Shoot," but I caught myself in time. "It's fine. I'm glad to talk to you." I turned the desk chair around for her to sit down, and I carefully closed the door.

"This is very hard for me." She rubbed her hand across her cheek. A diamond as large as my little fingernail winked and blinked. I remembered what Uncle Jeremiah had said about her jewels—that the third accident had been caused by someone intent on robbing the place. Had she been here then? What about the time before?

". . . my grandson." I realized she was finishing up. I'd been so engrossed in my speculations I hadn't heard the first part of the sentence.

"I'm sorry. I was focused on something else," I said. "I wasn't listening."

It turned out to have nothing to do with Uncle Jeremiah or my outbursts. She had a grandson who'd been crippled in a diving accident. She had some questions about the physical therapy he was undergoing—some concerns about how slow the progress was. She wanted my opinion.

I tried to be positive, to stress how kids especially could overcome tremendous odds.

"Have you always come at the same time of year?" I asked, determined that she wasn't going to leave without answering some of my questions.

"When my husband was alive we used to come in January—to get away from the Minnesota winter. After he died I began coming later—late April, early May."

I sucked in my breath. "Have you always come at the same time as Helena, Margot, and Dr. Morgansting?"

"Helena, yes. And Mr. and Mrs. Jamison." Her face relaxed in a tender smile. "The four of us used to play bridge." She shook her head. "Then Arthur died. . . ."

"Who else?" I prompted before she could get sidetracked.

"Chuckie's parents, Margot's parents. . . . No, wait a minute. Margot's parents stopped coming quite a while back. I don't think we were with them after '77 or '78. It's hard for me to remember exactly. Their Christmas cards stopped shortly after that as well." She sighed. "It was disappointing. I'd thought we were friends."

"But Margot has been here at the same time you have been?"

"Not always." She glanced down at her hand. "She doesn't have much money. Works as a file clerk, I think. Has only two weeks off a year."

Like a lot of us, I thought, realizing that for someone like Mrs. Bentley, who'd probably never worked, the idea of a limited vacation time was hard to comprehend.

"It wasn't always that way," Mrs. Bentley said. "The poor girl had an altercation with her parents. Some ugly business over a broken romance, I believe. They disowned her."

"I thought that sort of thing only happened in the movies."

"Oh, no. When there's lots of money and the family name at stake, it can be quite real. There was a time when Arthur was going to disown our son. But I was able to get him to wait. Sure enough, when Bill turned twenty-five, he settled down. Now he's a partner in my husband's former law firm. Well, my dear"—she stood up—"thank you for your encouragement. I hope you sleep well and that no more disturbing incidents happen to you. I was quite shocked this morning. Quite shocked."

She was out the door by the time I remembered she'd never answered about Dr. Morgansting. I got out the books and continued recording the names that reappeared at the same time. Dr. Morgansting, Helena, the Jamisons, and Mrs. Bentley did appear to stay here if not at completely the same time, overlapping a few days or a week.

I stiffened at the sound of footsteps. There was another quick succession of taps. Once again I shoved the books under the covers and went to the door. "Who is it?"

"It's Helena."

Helena? I opened the door. I felt a little nervous, unsure about the safety of letting her into my room and then closing the door. After all, *she* had been the one with the gun.

"May I come in for a moment?" she asked.

"Certainly." I held open the door, peering out into the blackness to reassure myself that others were about, I guess. Unfortunately I didn't see anyone. "How's your headache?"

"Better . . . no, actually, I didn't have an honest-to-goodness headache. I was upset. I've been thinking a lot today about certain things—things you've brought up that I myself have been concerned about."

We were both standing. Wordlessly I waved at the desk chair, and I took a seat on the bed, my knee accidentally pulling at the blanket and uncovering one of the books. Helena looked at it, looked as if she recognized it for what it was, but didn't comment. I bit my lip to keep from offering a massive free flow of explanations.

"I, too, think someone is out to harm Jeremiah."

There was a long silence. I was waiting for her to continue before I offered up any more information. I wasn't quite sure what she was waiting for. Even if she was the guilty one, this could be just a ruse to get me off guard. She could be pretending to join ranks.

As we were sitting there, we both heard the screen door open. The doorknob rattled. Helena's eyes widened. Someone was trying to get in—and not even being very secretive about it. I jumped off the bed and reached to unlock the door. Somehow having Helena here with me kept me from asking who was there and what was going on. I wanted to see who was there.

"'Scuse me, Ms. Nelson," a male voice said. "Just making sure your door was locked."

The scent of rose perfume surrounded me like a warm fog as Helena moved so that she was behind me. "Raymond?" she said sharply. "Is that you?"

"Yes, Ms. Knight. Mr. Sloane asked me to make extra rounds of the cottages. That's all. Didn't mean to alarm you." He put his hand to his hat. "Good night."

"Raymond, wait!" I called out.

He moved back into sight under the dim porch light.

"Could you dispose of that—please?" I pointed to the cottontail.

"Surely." He bent down.

"What is it?" Helena asked.

"A squashed cottontail."

"I'll take care of it for you, Ms. Nelson," Raymond said.

"Thank you." I shivered involuntarily and closed the door. "I found that lovely object in my suitcase today—along with a note warning me to MYOB."

"Really? Do you have the note?"

"It's here somewhere." I glanced around, trying to remember exactly what I'd done with it after I'd read it. I finally found it in the bottom of the wastebasket. I uncrumpled the note and handed it to Helena. She murmured the words out loud, shifted the paper, checking both the front and the back.

"Ring any bells?"

She glanced up. "No."

"It didn't for me, either."

"But it bears out our concern that someone is after Jeremiah and that that someone thinks you may get in the way." Helena caught the edge of her lower lip between her teeth and frowned at the note again.

I thought of finding the cottontail and shivered. "Knowing that Raymond's patrolling should reassure me. Why doesn't it?"

Helena put her arm around my shoulders and gave me a quick squeeze. "He just startled you, that's all. He startled me too."

"What will Raymond and the others do when the ranch closes?"

"There are plenty of dude ranches around. There are some in Tucson, Phoenix, Wickenburg. They're always looking for good employees."

"Do you think any of the employees would want to hurt Uncle Jeremiah?" I was feeling calmer. There was something about Helena's serene presence tonight that completely put to rest my former suspicions of her.

"No," she said slowly. "I think it's a guest." Her gaze met mine, her eyes dark, beautiful, and very serious.

"Who?"

She hesitated. "I'd rather not say until I have more information. I could be wrong, and if that were the case, I'd never forgive myself."

"I—"

A loud knock on the door made us both jump. "Good grief, this room is as busy as Grand Central Station! I'll get rid of whoever it is," I said. Helena had lost her composure. Looking frightened, she moved out of sight of the door.

"Who is it?" I asked.

"Donovan."

Helena moved toward me and put her hand on my arm. "It's all right. I don't mind if Donovan knows I'm here."

"Are you sure? I can ask him to leave."

She shook her head. "No, I've said all I feel comfortable saying. We can talk again tomorrow. There's something I want to do first."

"Judith," Donovan said, "is everything all right?"

"Yes. Just a second." I felt really torn—as if I were letting information get away, and yet I wanted to see Donovan. Alone.

Helena solved my dilemma by reaching past me and unlocking the door. "Hello, Donovan."

"I didn't mean to interrupt anything," he said.

"You didn't. I was just leaving. Good night," she said, turning a radiant smile on us both.

"You're my fourth visitor of the evening," I said. How were things between us? I scanned him. Was he in a good mood? Or still feeling upset over Rudy's phone call?

"About the phone call. . . ." we said in unison.

"I had no business acting the way I did," Donovan finished. "You have a right to talk to whomever you want or to do whatever you want."

"It feels important to me for you to know that my interest in Rudy is only as a nice guy—a friend. Nothing else."

Donovan looked at me intently for a moment and then murmured that he was glad to hear that. "I didn't ask you before if there was a guy in your life at home. Is there?"

"No. At least not anymore." I was amazed to discover that for the first time there wasn't a little jolt of pain when I admitted that. "I went out with a guy, Kevin Caldwell, for eighteen months. Then I discovered he was also dating an acquaintance of mine." I smiled ruefully. "So I stopped seeing him. It hurt. A lot. But I'm over it now," I said briskly. "So did you have a chance to interview any of the wranglers, or have you been with Uncle Jeremiah all this time?"

"I finished two more games with Jeremiah."

"Who won?"

"It was a split. Then I went to the bunkhouse. Mind if I sit down?"

I shook my head. He turned the desk chair backward and straddled it, putting his arms across the frame and resting his chin on them. I went over to my bed and sat down.

"Oscar and Raymond were both there. Raymond has worked for the ranch for fifteen years, Oscar for six. Neither of them has anything to gain by the ranch being sold. In fact, if anything, it will be hard for them." He went on to describe their versions of the so-called accidents, which pretty much paralleled what Uncle Jeremiah had told me. "One interesting thing cropped up. Raymond told me there'd been a fire here—in the office—years ago. I wondered if that could be linked."

"I don't think so. Uncle Jeremiah mentioned it too. Seems a wrangler he'd fired retaliated by trying to burn the place down."

"That's what Raymond said—a wrangler who had gotten involved with one of the guests. I guess that's against ranch policy."

"Which guest?"

"I didn't think to ask. It didn't seem relevant." He

pretended to shield his head against an attack. "Guess I wouldn't have made such a hot detective myself."

"Okay." I grinned. "I won't rub it in." I threw back the covers, showing the books and my list. "As far as I can tell, most of the guests here have come at just about the same time every year for years. The exceptions are Chuck and Susie and Margot. This is Chuck and Susie's first visit. Margot doesn't have much money, so she makes it only every two or three years and stays exactly two weeks. A lot of the other guests stay a *month*. Can you imagine how much that must cost?"

"No one here is living at the poverty level," Donovan said in a voice that implied he didn't altogether approve of the life-styles of the rich and famous.

"Except Margot. Her parents disowned her."

"Disowned her? That seems a bit extreme—considering Margot. She's so meek, malleable looking."

"I know. Wait a minute. Do you suppose—" I stopped. I could imagine it. . . . Margot falling in love with a wrangler, her parents horrified. But would they disown her—for that? No. It didn't wash. They'd just pack her up, go home, and never come back. Besides, at that time she must have been in her early teens.

"Are you thinking she might have been the one involved with the wrangler?" Donovan asked.

"No, she was probably too young. Uncle Jeremiah said the firing happened ten years ago."

"So she would have been fifteen or sixteen," Donovan said. "Could be her. Believe me, I know girls that age. They're vulnerable, easily convinced they're in love."

"I know. I was one once."

"To her parents it could have posed an incredible embarrassment," Donovan went on.

I opened and closed the books until I found April of 1977. Running my finger down the page, I let out a startled little squeak when I saw Mr. and Mrs. Minor Hill and Margot. "She was here, with her parents."

Quickly I flipped to the next year. I ran my fingers down ten pages, starting with late March and going through to when the ranch closed in May. No Hills were listed. Nor were they here the following year, or the next. It was only when I got to 1983 that Margot Hill was listed. Her parents never showed up again.

During my frantic search Donovan had gotten off the chair and come to stand next to me. He bent down his chin, brushing my hair, and studied the book with me. "Bingo," he said under his breath and pointed to Margot's tidy writing in April of 1983.

I looked up at him. "How will we find out if she was the girl? Helena," I answered before he could. "She came to tell me she was suspicious—that might explain why she was annoyed earlier with Margot." I frowned, trying to make sense of all the thoughts racing through my brain. "But why would Margot try to kill Uncle Jeremiah? I mean, they seem very fond of each other."

"Unrequited love? He fired the wrangler. She never got over it? Her parents disowned her, so she's come to take it out on the man who caused it?" Donovan didn't sound sure. He plunked down on the edge of the bed next to me.

"It just doesn't fit Margot's personality. That's the trouble. You heard Uncle Jeremiah saying at dinner how he picked up the dead rabbits to protect her feelings."

"And how she blushed and thanked him," Donovan finished for me. "I don't know, Judith. It does seem improbable. My money's on Rudy. He wants to scare Jeremiah into closing the ranch deal."

"Yes, but there's something else you should know about the cottontail business." Quickly I filled Donovan in on finding the dead rabbit and the note.

"The note was printed in large block printing. Maybe it isn't a coincidence that Margot printed her name in tiny letters here in the book."

"Do they match?"

As I went to pick the warning note off the desk, I realized it wasn't there. Nor was it in the wastebasket. "That's odd."

"What is?"

"The note isn't here. I showed it to Helena. I guess she accidentally took it with her." Accidentally—or did she plan to show it to Margot? Or was she destroying evidence?

"Let's try to find out the name of the compromised guest. Someone around here has to know."

"I'll try Lupita," I said.

"I'll ask the wranglers. In the meantime warn Jeremiah. And watch Margot."

"She's going on the ride in the morning." I lifted my shoulders and made a face. "I wish I weren't. I think I'm going to regret this. I don't care for horses."

"You'll be fine. I'll be there to help keep an eye on Margot . . . and you. Jeremiah will be here. Rudy? Where's he going to be? Do you know?"

"Tucson—that should take him most of the day." I

took a deep breath. "Oh, Donovan, for the first time I feel as if we're on to something!"

"I do too." The serious expression had left his face. He was smiling. "I'm also looking forward to the breakfast ride and just being with you. I've found since you've come I look forward to every morning. I can hardly concentrate on my work. All I want is to be with you."

"What a lovely thing to say!"

"What about you? How are you feeling about me?" Donovan held out his arms, and I moved into them as if it were the most natural thing in the world.

My arms slipped around him. I could feel the strength of his back beneath the softness of his shirt. "Don't you know? Can't you tell?"

He kissed my closed eyes, my cheeks, his lips at last finding mine.

"Oh, Donovan," I murmured.

He held me a little away. "A complaint?" he whispered, his eyes tender. He pulled me against him again, hugging me. I could hear his heart, his breathing.

Swamped with feelings of excitement and what felt like a deep rush of love, I tipped my face up to study him. "I never dreamed it was possible to feel this way," I said. "I'm a little afraid. I think I may be falling in love with you. How can that be? We hardly know each other."

My words were caught up in another kiss. A kiss that told me Donovan was feeling the same wild, exciting feelings I was and that it didn't matter. All that mattered was that we *had* found each other. So I si-

lenced the questions and gave myself to the moment
and our shared kiss.

Donovan touched the top of my head, smoothing
my hair back. I tipped my face up, and he kissed me
quickly on the lips. "It's late."

"I'm glad you stopped by."

"Me too." His hand caressed the curve of my
cheek. His eyes behind the wire-rimmed glasses were
warm. We kissed again. Then he got to his feet.
"Sleep tight. And keep your door locked."

I assured him I would do both.

CHAPTER NINE

As it turned out, I didn't sleep well at all. Twice I woke with a start, thinking that I heard a noise —either someone trying to get into my room or someone outside my window. But when I lifted the gauzy curtain and peered out, I couldn't see anything except cacti outlined by the moon's glow and the black monstrous shape of Silver Dome. Off in the distance an occasional coyote howled. At two A.M. I turned on the light for an hour and read my mystery book until I felt sleepy again.

In the morning I went straight to the kitchen. Lupita, her cheeks flushed from the heat of the stove, was frying mounds of bacon. I quizzed her about the wrangler.

"His last name was Burr—that's all I know, señorita." She spoke sharply in Spanish to Conception. The little girl was in the pantry searching for something among the stacks of cans.

"Do you know why he was fired?" I asked Lupita.

Conception thumped a giant can of applesauce on

the counter and flashed me a shy smile. Lupita
thanked her and shooed her outside. She waited until
Conception was out of sight before she answered. "He
was caught with one of the guests."

"Which guest?"

"I don't know. Señor Sloane would never gossip
about a guest. When Señor Sloane found out, he had
Burr's bedroll in the back of the truck before daybreak. That is what Raymond told me." She cocked
her head to one side and looked intently at me.

"And what about the fire? When did that happen?"

"The very next night. Someone set a wastebasket in
the office on fire. It did some damage before it was
discovered. Señor Sloane suspected it was Burr."

"Did he see him?"

She shook her head. "No. It was during the dinner
hour. After the fire your uncle hired someone to be at
the desk. But that was a long time ago, señorita. Why
all these questions? What has that got to do with
Señor Sloane now?"

"I don't know—exactly." I couldn't very well say
that we thought it could be Margot . . . or Rudy. After
all, Rudy was related to her, and we had no proof.
"Donovan and I are afraid maybe Margot Hill may
want to hurt my uncle."

If I'd thought Lupita would be upset about Donovan's suspicion of Rudy, I was totally unprepared for
her reaction to Margot's name. Her eyes rounded; her
hand flew up to her lips. "No," she said, shaking her
head hard. "Señorita Hill would not hurt anybody.
She's—" Lupita's voice broke off as she searched for
a word. "She's like a child in many ways. She would
not hurt Señor Sloane. You must be mistaken."

She seemed so positive, I could feel my own doubts building like thunderclouds. "In any case, please don't let her or anyone be alone with my uncle. Margot will be on this morning's ride, so I don't need to worry."

"I will be at Vilagos, too, señorita. The food needs someone to serve it. That someone is me . . . and Alice, my cousin, will help. But it will be all right. Conception is going to take Señor Sloane his tray at nine. I will ask her to sit outside his door and color the pictures in her book. Don't worry. He will be fine."

I counted eleven horses saddled and waiting in the corral at the stable. Donovan was leaning against the split-wood railing, watching me, I realized. When he saw that I saw him, he pried himself away and strolled toward me. "You ought to see the expression on your face."

"Enthusiastic?"

"Hardly." He put his hand on the back of my neck and shook it gently. "You aren't riding a stallion, you know. Just an overfed gelding who's used to walking in a long, slow line—that is, I'm assuming from your comments last night that you're going on the beginner's ride."

"If I could, I'd choose a beginner's beginner."

Donovan chuckled. His fingers curled deliciously around the base of my neck, rubbing the tenseness away. "Discover anything?" he whispered, bending so that his lips touched my ear.

"Not a whole lot. The wrangler's name was Burr. He was caught in a delicate moment with a guest. But Lupita didn't know or wouldn't say who the guest was. She definitely doesn't think Margot's a threat to Uncle Jeremiah. Even I'm beginning to have doubts. She doesn't seem the type."

We both glanced at Margot. She was already seated on a bay horse that was giving her a bad time, throwing his head back, prancing. She stayed calm, bending forward slightly in the saddle to pat his neck and to talk quietly. Dr. Morgansting, sitting straight as a Prussian officer, was on a delicate-looking black horse. Beside him Helena prepared to mount. She stuck her left boot in a stirrup, grasped the saddlehorn, and swung effortlessly onto a palomino. The saddle she was using looked as if it were encrusted with real silver.

Donovan's hands moved to my tense shoulder muscles, kneading them. It felt wonderful.

"Have you ever thought of doing physical therapy on the side?" I asked, leaning into the pleasant strength of his massage.

"No, but I have been thinking along a similar line."

"What?"

"I've been thinking how nice a nature camp for physically disabled kids would be. A physical therapist—like you," he added, smiling, "could work with their muscles, while a teacher like me could explain desert lore, conservation, and nature study."

"What a neat idea! I wonder if anyone has done such a thing."

"I don't know. We could form a partnership and buy the Silver Sands."

The fantasy took hold. I could almost see us. . . . "Wait a minute. I'm a city woman, remember?"

"Actually, I'd forgotten. With your hair pulled into

a ponytail like that, wearing faded jeans and a sweat-shirt, you look completely at home."

"I feel like a visitor. I like tall buildings. . . ."

"There's always Silver Dome. It's tall."

I glanced across the corral at the stark, purple mountain. Unfortunately it repelled rather than at-tracted me. "Not the same. Besides, I like grass. Flowers."

"The desert has flowers—all the cacti are ripe and ready to go. All we need is some rain."

"Slow riders," Oscar called out.

"That's you," Donovan said. "Your horse is the one tied to the water trough. His name is Concho."

Concho was small and so fat he looked as if he were a toy. "I think I can manage him. You figured if I wanted to stop, I could just drag my feet on the ground. Right?"

"We could switch. You could ride the horse I'm exercising."

"Which one is that?"

"Apache. Your uncle's horse."

"I can imagine what he's like. No, thanks. I'll stick to Fatty here." *ATVs yesterday, horses today, probably a rocket to the moon tomorrow,* I thought.

"Here." Donovan dropped two lumps of sugar into my hand. "These should cement your friendship."

"How sweet. Thanks."

"Hold your hand flat," Donovan admonished.

But every time I saw Concho's raised upper lip and those teeth, my fingers curled up of their own accord. Finally Donovan held my fingers down for me. Ever so nicely, Concho lipped the sugar off the palm of my hand.

I stroked Concho's rose-petal-soft nose. "I think you made a good selection," I said. "Thank you."

"Time to get on board." Donovan laced his fingers together to form a cup for me to put my left foot in. Not wanting to feel too heavy, I threw my right leg over the horse, flinging the weight of my body after it. I would have slid right off the other side if Donovan hadn't grabbed my leg and pulled me back. There were a few good-humored chuckles.

Oscar had me lift my feet from the stirrups and adjusted the length until it was comfortable. Because Concho was so broad, my feet were farther from the ground than I'd thought they'd be.

Donovan disappeared into the stable. Moments later he reappeared on the back of a prancing pinto with gleaming brown eyes and a swishing tail. Obviously Donovan had been on a horse many times; he looked completely at home.

"I don't want to slow you down," I said, remembering yesterday and how I'd outrun him. Today he was going to outride me—that was for sure. "You don't have to ride with me. I'll be fine."

"But I want to ride with you." He fell into line behind me. Susie, riding a nondescript brown horse, and Chuck, who was on a horse that could have been Concho's twin, moved into line behind him; then the Jamisons' son and daughter-in-law joined us.

There was a cool breeze; the sky was an azure blue with large clouds building on the horizon. It promised to be a beautiful day; Concho's slow walk held the promise of a peaceful journey. Within moments I was relaxed enough to enjoy the winding trail and the scenery.

Almost an hour later after going up and down, seemingly to circle back where we started, we suddenly began climbing a steep, narrow, rocky hill. I leaned forward in the saddle, trying to help Concho, whose labored breathing let me know this wasn't his idea of fun.

As we slipped over the top, a ragged town came into view and I caught my breath. There were half a dozen rickety wooden buildings that seemed to cling to the sides of the mountain. In the small cleared area, formerly the main street, I guessed, there was an old saloon, a two-story hotel, and several houses.

"Vilagos, what's left of it," Donovan said. "Good. There's the cook wagon. I'm starving."

The cook wagon, which was a pickup truck from the ranch, was filled with covered pans of various sizes. Lupita and her cousin were feeding a cook fire that had been built in a pit circled with rocks. One of the wranglers—Raymond, I guessed since he was wearing a red apron that had *Don't Mess With Ray* on the front of it—was jiggling a frying pan over the fire. It was filled with potatoes, onions, and scrambled eggs. The people on the fast ride were already in line for food.

"How does the truck get up here?" I couldn't imagine anything traveling up the steep, narrow trail we'd been on.

"There's a back route," Donovan said. "Not great but manageable. Since you have to drive partially around the mountain, it takes quite a bit longer than just going directly from the ranch by horse." He got off his horse, throwing the reins down. The pinto nosed the ground and moved a few feet away from us.

"Won't he run away?"

"No, he'll be fine." Donovan held up his arms to me. I swung my leg over and slid off, once again misjudging the distance and nearly knocking us both over. "Sorry. Grace is not my middle name."

"That's okay. I never know what to expect from you. It's challenging—exciting."

Donovan and I took plates and got in line to have them filled up with tantalizing food. At Donovan's urging we sat beneath a ledge. The ground was still damp and cool, while the sun provided a lazy, cozy warmth on our faces.

Helena sat between Chuck and Susie, regaling them with stories of the old place. Margot never sat down that I saw. Carrying her plate, taking quick, anxious bites, she strolled around, keeping her eyes focused on the ground, occasionally bending to pick something up. Dr. Morgansting shared bits of his breakfast with his horse. Mrs. Jamison and some of the others sat in the shade of a ramshackle building and chatted. After we ate and had coffee, most of us lay half asleep, like sunning lizards, on the flat rocks.

"Want to look around?" Donovan asked after a while.

"I do, but I don't know if I can move."

Donovan extended his hand and pulled me to my feet. Hand in hand we walked through the shell of a town.

Most of the buildings were boarded up, and we couldn't get inside. Jeremiah had had them sealed to keep guests from getting injured, Donovan told me. Just as he'd tried to seal up the old mine. Naturally

curious, a lot of the guests didn't realize how dangerous it could be.

"It looks like a movie set," I said.

"Have you been to Old Tucson?" he asked.

"No."

"It's an old movie set—preserved. Maybe we can
go there."

"Maybe. There isn't much time left." A sudden
pang made me realize that if I got much more involved with Donovan, saying good-bye to him was
going to be hard—very hard.

As if he were having the same thoughts, Donovan
reached for my hand, lacing his strong, calloused
fingers through mine. Suddenly there seemed to be an
aching sadness between us.

As we slowly sauntered back toward the group,
Donovan pointed out where the abandoned silver mine
was.

"I went up to look at it once," Helena said. "It's a
haul and not much to see, but it's a pity it closed down
and Vilagos with it."

"Why did it?" I asked.

"The vein petered out. Then there was a cholera
outbreak. People got suspicious of the well water.
They upped stakes and left—almost overnight. It
happened to a lot of mining towns."

"I used to think there were ghosts sleeping in the
hotel and that if I came here at night, I could see them
flying out the windows," Margot volunteered. Then
she blushed fiercely, as if that had been a childish
thing to say.

I glanced at the hotel, a tall, flimsy-looking struc-
ture with a funny phony balcony over the front door

and, beneath it, an old weatherbeaten sign hanging by part of a rusty chain. On the second floor the glassless windows gaped like blinded eyes. I could see what Margot meant. It was really scary looking. I'd have thought the same thing as a kid—maybe even as an adult.

"I wouldn't care to spend a night here—that's for sure," I said.

Margot didn't comment. Her moment of friendliness to me on the porch last night had disappeared, never to resurface. *Strange woman,* I thought. She and Helena hadn't seemed to patch up their difference, either. Although they were near each other, they barely spoke. Helena was acting like a tour leader, pointing out objects of interest to the guests, while Margot seemed lost in her own thoughts.

"Time to mount up," Raymond called out. The truck had been loaded up and had headed back to the ranch. Mrs. Bentley had hitched a ride. Her horse would just be led back by one of the wranglers. If Donovan hadn't been there, I would have been tempted to ask if I could do the same. A little riding went a long way.

Helena and Margot mounted in a jiffy. Dr. Morgansting took his time tightening his cinch. I realized that, in the confusion of leading horses around and the muddle of people mounting, anyone who knew what he or she was doing could secretly cut a cinch with a sharp knife.

Donovan led Concho toward me.

"Do I have to?" I asked, teasing.

I don't know why we didn't hear them sooner. Perhaps it was because of the confusion of the chatter and mounting—but suddenly there was a roar, and out of nowhere two dirt bikes jumped over the ridge into the middle of us. They seemed headed straight for me. Instinctively I slammed into Donovan, who was blocking me with both hands. The reins jerked out of his hands as Concho whinnied and threw his head.

Caught off balance, Donovan stumbled forward and fell down. Susie, who'd been just about to get on her horse, went flying backward as the horse reared up. I saw the wild, rolling eyes of her horse, its hooves swiping through the air. Susie screamed and fell. Somewhere a wrangler was shouting, "Whoa! Whoa!" I moved out of the way as a runaway horse bolted straight toward me.

As quickly as they'd appeared, the bikers disappeared. Donovan staggered to his feet and took off after them.

I went to Susie, who didn't look injured, although she seemed to be having trouble catching her breath. *Hyperventilating,* some part of me assessed. Gently I pushed her forward to collapse her tight diaphragm. "Slow your breathing," I said. "Take a long, deep breath and let it out slowly."

"I can't!" she gasped. "I—I can't breathe. I—"

"Is she *dying?*" Chuck kneeled beside me, grabbing Susie's hand in his. "Somebody, help!"

"I *am* helping her. It's all right. She'll be okay."

Susie rolled her eyes up; her mouth opened and closed in pitiful attempts to get more air.

I looked around for what I needed and couldn't find it. "Why don't you give me your shirt?" I said to Chuck. "Maybe that will work."

Chuck unbuttoned his shirt and handed it to me.

Gathering it into a pouch, my fingers holding the top tight except for a small opening, I held it against Susie's nose and mouth. "Breathe into this," I said. "Take a deep breath and let it out slowly."

Susie fought me at at first; then gradually she did as I instructed, and within five minutes the obvious panic had disappeared and she was breathing normally, her face rosy pink. When I took the shirt away, the tears came. She clung to Chuck, sobbing.

Donovan reappeared, his face red. His shirt had been ripped down one side. "Is she all right?"

"Yes. Just upset." Now that the emergency was over, I could feel my muscles tensing.

"They got away," he said. "Wait till I get my hands on Rudy! They had to come from his place. That irresponsible—"

He was interrupted by shouts from the wranglers. Two of the horses had been scared off. Raymond asked if Donovan would mount up and help them. The rest of us regrouped and went to sit in the shade. In the confusion of the moment it had completely escaped me that Margot and Helena and Dr. Morgansting had disappeared.

Panicked, I looked around. Had they gone with Donovan and the wranglers? Or had they gone back to the ranch? I asked several of the others, but everybody was in a state of confusion. Nobody seemed to know. There was nothing I could do except sit and worry.

It seemed to take forever, but finally Donovan, Oscar, and Raymond reappeared with the horses. The runaways were blowing air through their nostrils, their shoulders and flanks lathered. I immediately went to Donovan and told him my concern.

"The three of them are together. If Helena's as concerned as you said last night, let's hope she keeps an eye open."

I hadn't thought of that. It made sense and I felt easier.

No one could induce Susie to get back on her horse. Finally Donovan offered to walk back with her. On horseback themselves, the two wranglers led the two riderless horses.

Rudy's ATV was in front of the main building. What was he doing here, I wondered. He'd said last night he was going to Tucson. I hurried up to the main lodge. Just seeing the ATV brought back my feelings of outrage at this morning's catastrophe. Donovan was right. ATVs had no place on the desert. One of us could have been killed today.

I caught a glimpse of Margot carrying a pitcher of water, heading into her room. That was a relief. In the hallway a faint scent of rose perfume lingered. So Helena had been nearby. Maybe, as Donovan had suggested, she was watching Margot. As I went into the living room, I stopped short. Rudy was speaking, and from the sound of his voice, he was angry. "That's it, then. You won't reconsider?"

I edged into the room.

"No. My mind's made up. My decision is final."

"You'll regret it!" Rudy clenched his hands but propelled himself away from the couch and toward the door, nearly colliding with me. His face was dark with rage. He glanced at me and passed right on by, not speaking.

I hurried after him, catching him just outside the door. "Rudy, wait."

"Now what?" He folded his arms and surveyed me, his eyes flat, the pleasant teasing of our last few times together gone. This was a side of him I'd never seen, and I didn't like it.

"Listen, a terrible thing happened today at breakfast. Two dirt bikers roared into camp and terrified the horses. Donovan and I were nearly run over. Susie's horse reared, and she fell off. The worst part is, the bikers didn't even stop to see if anybody was hurt. They just kept right on going."

"Where were you?"

"At Vilagos."

"The dirt-bike trail veers off before it gets there. It's plainly marked."

"Rudy, they roared into camp, catching us completely by surprise."

"Did you get a look at the bikers?"

I shook my head. "It happened too fast."

He sighed, running his hands through his hair. "I'll check into it. I'll ask Max. . . ." He peered at me, a softer look on his face. "Nothing happened to you, did it?"

"No. It shook me up, though."

"Donovan?"

"He's okay. He just suffered a ripped shirt."

"That's too bad." The fierce anger was back, sharpening his eyes, narrowing his wide mouth. "You can tell him for me that I'm sick of the lies he's feeding Jeremiah. I can't believe it. Everything was going so well. Then Donovan . . . then you. . . ."

"Me? What have I done?"

"It's more what you haven't done."

I caught his unspoken thoughts as if he'd said them.

"Oh, you mean I didn't browbeat Uncle Jeremiah into selling *you* the land?"

Rudy threw up his hands as if I were a hopeless case and stormed past me.

With effort I controlled my own anger. Uncle Jeremiah was my concern, not Rudy.

Uncle Jeremiah's face was very pale. Sitting next to him, on the edge of the couch, I took his hand, letting my fingers slide to his wrist, searching for his pulse. His breathing was harsh, fast. Through the half-opened window I heard Rudy's ATV spring to life and roar away. I glanced at my watch. Uncle Jeremiah's pulse was a little rapid but not bad for someone who'd just been in a violent argument.

"What was that all about?" I asked.

"I told Rudy I wouldn't sell him Silver Sands. It didn't go down very well. I also told him that even if I didn't sell to anyone, I wasn't going to lease the foot-hill land to him anymore. He has to look elsewhere for his ATV park." He paused to take quick, shallow breaths.

No wonder Rudy had been so upset. I felt sorry . . . and glad.

Uncle Jeremiah shook his head. "I just can't see those darn buzzing, dirt-kicking things running all over Silver Sands. The idea of it offends my sensibility."

If he knew what had gone on at Silver Dome, it would really upset him. There was no point in telling him until he was more relaxed, though. I patted his arm, aware of the way his increased heartbeat was pulsating in his thin neck. "Do you want me to get your inhaler?" My own breathing was out of sync with my words. My earlier deduction about Margot's guilt seemed to be crumbling around the edges.

He shook his head. "No. I'll be all right. I used it about twenty minutes ago."

As I sat with Uncle Jeremiah, Rudy's outraged statement, "You'll regret it," played over and over in my mind. There'd been a force, a threat behind those words that couldn't be overlooked. And I couldn't rid my mind of the idea that everything that had happened to me since my arrival here had somehow happened right after I'd been with Rudy.

The pill could have been inserted hastily into a muffin. Rudy could have taken a shot at Donovan and me. He could even have put the squashed cottontail in my suitcase. He could even have had the bikers terrorize the breakfast ride this morning, I realized with a fresh sense of outrage. That would keep us all busy while he came here and harassed Uncle Jeremiah.

Maybe what had happened in the past had been accidents, while everything that had happened recently was simply an act of terrorism directed by one greedy man who was willing to use any methods to get an older man to sell his land to him. Maybe Rudy had thought that if he could scare me, I'd convince Uncle Jeremiah that staying here was dangerous, so he'd sell more quickly.

"What are you thinking?" Uncle Jeremiah asked.

"That you made the right decision. The Silver Sands is much too beautiful to be turned into an ATV park."

"They're the cause of too many accidents, too many people being killed." He let out a long, low sigh. "If only I could go back twenty years—be young, healthy! I'd never leave this place."

"Couldn't you get some young couple to come in —help you?"

Uncle Jeremiah opened his eyes and peered at me intently. "How about you staying here?"

"Me?" The idea was so preposterous, I giggled nervously. "I don't know the first thing about operating a ranch."

"Donovan and I had a little chat over backgammon last night."

So that was why he'd brought the idea up this morning at the corral. "Oh, did you? He thought I ought to come here and help you run the ranch, did he?" I smiled, pleased that Donovan cared enough to bring up such a silly idea; at the same time, I was aware once again of a sadness at the thought of leaving him.

"What if we turned the place into a special ranch for kids—kids with physical problems?" Uncle Jeremiah said. "They could come here with their parents for one or two weeks. You could work with them. Donovan could show them nature things."

"I know. Donovan's already explained that to me. He neglected to tell me what you'd do," I gently teased. Uncle Jeremiah's pulse continued to improve as his medicine took effect and he calmed down.

"Why, around the nightly campfire, I'd tell them stories of the old days. I'd be the resident granddad."

"I must have gotten too much sun today," I said, getting to my feet slowly. "For a second there I could see everything you just outlined. For a moment I actually considered it possible. No, I can't do it,

Uncle Jeremiah. I'm a city girl. You'd better go right on with your plans to sell the place if you don't want to run it. Don't make up fantasies that include me— especially fantasies that link me up to a man I've known for not quite two days."

"Keep an open mind, Judith," he called after me. "And take a good look around outside. The desert has a funny way of latching on to your heart."

And so do some of the inhabitants, I thought against my will. *Two men in particular.*

CHAPTER TEN

The rest of the day was uneventful. I'd hoped Donovan would come by when he and Susie got to the ranch, but he didn't. I took a nap, waking when long, purple shadows slipped down the white wall. Behind Silver Dome an orange sunset was already underway. By the time I'd showered and pressed the wrinkles out of my blue cotton dress with the little travel iron Mom had given me, the first dinner bell had sounded. I pulled on a pair of blue suede flats instead of heels and headed out into the warm air, carefully locking my door behind me.

Tonight I sat between Mr. Jamison and Susie. Uncle Jeremiah was resting in his room, Helena informed me. She was at the head of the table. There was going to be a bingo game tonight, she announced. Raymond had agreed to call numbers. She hoped everybody would play.

So I did, and lost five dollars. In between playing my card and wondering where Donovan was and what he was doing and missing his company, I watched the

other guests. Margot played three cards simultane-
ously and won small amounts twice. A shy, pleased
smile played over her lips.

What had she looked like as a fifteen-year-old? I
narrowed my eyes so that I couldn't see her present
image so clearly. At fifteen her thinness probably gave
her a touching delicacy. That, combined with those
large, sad eyes half hidden by the sweeping long
lashes, might well attract an intense love interest.

Money would be an added plus. It was obvious that
no one here knew what it was like to be poor. Money,
I suspected, was the real reason behind not letting the
help get romantically involved with the guests. It
would be too easy for someone lonely and vulnerable
to get set up. I couldn't help noticing that Margot
wore an aura of loneliness.

Helena played two games and then disappeared to
make a phone call and never returned. Mrs. Bentley
won the biggest jackpot. I watched Margot to see if
there was envy or greed reflected on her face. Quite
the contrary. She jumped up and hugged Mrs. Bentley. It was truly baffling. She seemed sweet, vulnerable. The idea of her wanting to hurt Uncle Jeremiah,
maybe even to kill him, seemed absurd.

I tried to telephone Mom again before I went to
bed, and got hold of Eddie instead. Mom was at a
PTA meeting. She'd told him to send me a hug if I
called and to remind me to be sure to wear plenty of
sunscreen. He told me he'd placed second in a swim-
ming meet. I told him about the trout Donovan had
caught and about riding an ATV. He was suitably impressed.

"Ask Mom to call me tomorrow, will you?" I said.
"I want to talk to her."

He promised he would.

Back in my room, I went through the ledgers again,
wondering if there was something in them I was missing. No matter how I jiggled the names and dates,
Margot continued to look like the prime suspect, although Rudy ran a close second. He'd been so angry
this afternoon. I hoped he'd finish his work on Matilda, and I wondered briefly what I'd do if he didn't.
Ask Donovan, I guessed. I wondered again why Donovan had simply disappeared. Was he checking on a
lead? Doing work around his place? I smiled to myself. Maybe he was sitting in front of a roaring campfire, stitching his torn shirt.

Pushing the curtain aside, I looked out at the blue-
black sky, at the thousand stars, at the pale moon. If I
weren't afraid of what I'd find out there, I'd have
been tempted to pay Donovan a visit. No, I'd finish
the book I'd chosen and turn in early.

In the morning I wasn't surprised to find another
Do Not Disturb sign on Uncle Jeremiah's door.
Knowing how weak he'd appeared yesterday after the
confrontation with Rudy, I thought it was a good idea
that he take it easy. Not that I was going to be lulled
into being careless. I'd double-check with Lupita that
he was in his room and that he was eating. Maybe if
there was a tactful way, I'd suggest that she ask Rudy
not to badger him about the land.

Not too many people had made it into the dining
room yet; I could sit anywhere I wanted to. Just as I
was putting my napkin in my lap, Donovan appeared.

He took the chair next to mine, touching me briefly on the shoulder, smiling at me.

"I missed you last night," I said.

"I missed you too. That biker incident turned out to have bigger consequences than I realized at the time."

"Really? What?"

"The horse Susie was riding injured its foreleg quite badly. And Oscar, when we were rounding up the runaways, got caught on some barbed wire. Got a nasty gash. He's got to go in to get it stitched up today."

"That's too bad."

"Anyway, I went back to the site with Raymond to see if we could catch the bikers coming down—but we didn't. I planned to see you before you went to bed, but by the time I did what I needed to around my place and here, there weren't any lights on in your room. I didn't want to wake you. Did you sleep well?"

"Actually, I did. I think the fresh air, the excitement of yesterday, and getting used to the time change all connected at once. I don't remember even dreaming."

"Your face got a lot of color yesterday. It makes your eyes look silvery—beautiful."

"Thank you."

"Good morning, Mrs. Bentley," Donovan said, getting up quickly.

"No—no, sit down. I can seat myself."

But Donovan was beside her, pulling out a chair for her and easing it to the table.

"Good morning, Judith," Mrs. Bentley said. "It's going to be a gloriously hot day today. I'll bet it gets over a hundred."

Helena strode in through the doorway and stopped.

She was wearing exactly the same outfit she'd been wearing the other day—the day I'd seen her with the gun—and her expression was tense. When she caught my gaze, she jerked her head. Wordlessly I pointed at Donovan. She nodded.

"Helena wants to speak with us," I whispered, and we excused ourselves and followed Helena into the living room.

"I'm very concerned," she said. "I'm afraid Margot—" She stopped and clasped her hands together. "I've befriended Margot for years, as you may know. She was rather like the daughter I never had. I really cared about her." She stopped speaking and blinked back tears. "Margot hasn't had an easy life, and she's a person who came into the world not very well defended. She needed a mother's love."

I could feel Donovan shift impatiently beside me, and I guessed that he was longing for her to get to the point. I hoped he wouldn't push. This sounded like the background information I'd been wishing for.

"Her mother never wanted children, and she treated Margot accordingly. But that's in the past, and there's no point in dwelling on it," Helena went on. "Anyway, Margot has been acting very odd this vacation. I've found her creeping around at all hours. One moment she seems like the old Margot; the next moment it's as if I don't know her. Rapid personality changes —and often upsetting ones. . . ."

Her voice faded away, and when she spoke again her train of thought had shifted. "I took the note you showed me, Judith, and I confronted her. She denied writing it, but she got very nervous. Then there's the matter of the ladder. The day Jeremiah had his accident, I saw Margot running from the direction of the cottage. Later, when I asked her why she hadn't gotten help for Jeremiah since she must have seen him fall, she denied having left her room."

"Where is she this morning?" Donovan asked.

"She didn't come in to breakfast." My heartbeat was picking up; a funny tickle started at the base of my throat.

"I saw her earlier," Helena said, "dressed as if she were going for her early-morning walk. She should be back at any moment. That's why I wanted to catch you first."

"Were you with her the other morning? The morning of the gunshot?"

"No. I knocked on her door before I left, but there was no answer. I have no idea whether she was sleeping or if she'd gone already."

"But you were walking. You had your gun. I saw you."

Donovan nudged me.

Helena saw him and quickly looked at me. "So you thought . . . you think. . . ."

"No—I mean, I did at first. But Donovan assured me your gun couldn't blast a cactus that way."

"No wonder you looked at me so strangely," Helena said. "Well, I didn't shoot at you."

"Could it have been Margot?"

"I know she knows how to shoot. Whether she has a gun with her or not, I've never asked. I haven't seen one. But you know there are guns—rifles—in a case in the tack house. Anybody could probably take one of those briefly, and no one would notice or comment."

"Breakfast!" Dr. Morgansting stuck his head in the doorway.

"Why would Margot do this?" I asked as the three of us obediently trailed toward the door. "I mean, I think I know why; I just need you to confirm it. Did she fall in love with a wrangler?"

"How did you know that?" Helena stopped. "She never— Jeremiah told you, I guess."

"No, we figured it out from information and from looking at the guest ledgers."

"Ah, yes. I saw the ledgers in your room and wondered. So you put two and two together."

"I think so. That's what I want you to tell me."

"I don't know much. There was an involvement with a wrangler. Jeremiah fired him. The whole mess caused a rift between Margot and her family, and Margot's family and Jeremiah. Her parents never came back here. After a few years Margot began coming alone. I think Jeremiah has felt guilty about that. I know he reduces the price for her. He's quite protective of her, you know. He won't hear a word against her. I've tried to warn him this time that I think she may have mental problems. He just changed the subject."

"Then we'll just have to watch and wait and catch her doing something suspicious," I said. "We need more proof than we have now to make anything stick."

"It feels a little like playing Russian roulette," Donovan observed. "But I think you're right."

When Margot hadn't appeared by the end of breakfast, Helena went to look for her. "What'll we do if she isn't around?" I asked Donovan.

"Check Jeremiah's room. Post a guard outside until we locate her."

Helena reappeared. "We can relax. She's in the shower," she said. "I heard her singing. I'll try to keep a close eye on her. If she's the culprit, this won't go on much longer. She's scheduled to leave in two more days."

I hadn't known that. "That means if she's going to do anything else, she'll have to move fast," I said.

"Or give up," Donovan pointed out. "If we can keep him safe two more days, it's clear sailing."

"What are you doing today? Will you be around?" I asked him.

"Yes, but unfortunately, since Oscar is going to the doctor, I promised Raymond I'd help shoe some of the horses. That'll take up all morning, possibly even this afternoon. But I'll be at the corral if you need me." He got to his feet, squeezed the back of my neck, sending pleasant tingles down my spine. He promised to see me at lunch and left.

Half waiting for Margot to put in an appearance, I lingered over another cup of coffee. Conception darted through the swinging door and began clearing the table. Soon Lupita appeared, carrying an empty tray. She seemed surprised to see me. "I hope you are satisfied with your car," she said.

"My car?" I looked at her blankly. "Rudy has my car."

"Then you haven't seen his surprise." She smiled broadly. Conception moved over so that she was leaning against her mother's hip and smiled at me, too, a perfect miniature of her mother.

"You mean he's fixed it? It's back?"

"Yes. He came very early this morning. He wanted you to see it first thing."

"I guess I was so involved with getting to breakfast I walked right by it. That's wonderful. I wish he'd stuck around. I need to pay him for the parts—thank him."

She shook her head. "He knew you would say that. He said it's on him—that he's sorry for yesterday?" Lupita posed the last part of the sentence as a question, as if she weren't entirely clear what it meant.

"We had a few cross words," I said, diluting the truth a little.

As we talked, Lupita had started clearing the table. "He is upset that Señor Sloane won't sell him the ranch."

"Yes, I know. How do you feel?"

She shrugged. "I hope Señor Sloane will keep the place. If he has to sell, then I hoped Rudy would be the buyer. But what will be will be."

"Well, I'm going to see my car. Maybe I'll drive up and see Rudy and thank him myself." Now I was the one beginning to feel guilty about yesterday—and my suspicions. I'd placed too much emphasis on what had simply been an outburst of temper. Rudy had made no bones about wanting to buy the ranch. To learn there was no possibility must have hurt. Then to be confronted by me about the bikers must have been the final straw. Anyone could have a temper tantrum. I'd certainly had a few that continued to haunt me from time to time.

Just in the hour I'd been at breakfast, the day had heated up. A blast of hot air greeted me, and a scorching sun blinded me. Shading my eyes, I looked around for Matilda. Maybe Rudy had parked the car out in back, near the kitchen. I walked around the building. The ranch station wagon was there, but heaven only knew where the keys were. The truck was down at the corral, wedged between the stable and corral, the back loaded with horse-shoeing equipment. No Matilda.

I stuck my head in the kitchen door. "Lupita? Where did Rudy leave my car? I can't find it."

Lupita looked up from the pan she was scrubbing. "In front of the main lodge, señorita."

"No—no, it isn't there."

"I saw it." Wiping her hands on her apron, her face knotted with concern, Lupita followed me outside. Together we hurried around to the front of the building. Her mouth fell open. "I don't understand. It was right there." She pointed to a spot right by the sidewalk. I glanced back. It was almost directly parallel to Uncle Jeremiah's room.

"Have you taken Uncle Jeremiah his breakfast tray?"

"Not yet. At nine o'clock. He prefers to wait until the guests are through and the kitchen less busy."

I'd already turned and was walking rapidly toward his room. Lupita bobbed after me. When we reached Uncle Jeremiah's door, I knocked and knocked again. On the third knock I turned the knob, and the door swung open. At first glance everything looked all right. He appeared to be asleep. But when I went over to the bed, I discovered that there were two sofa pillows beneath the bedcovers.

"Oh, no!" Lupita whispered.

On the nightstand beside the bed were the two different inhalers that contained prescription medicine for his breathing. There was a glass of water and several tablets. I picked one up and recognized that it was aspirin with codeine. I wasn't sure what finding these meant—whether Margot had tried to drug him and failed—or succeeded. I suspected that she'd gotten some inside him, enough to make it easy to move him. Perhaps the most ominous sight was the empty wheelchair next to the bed.

"Who would do such a thing?" Lupita asked.

"Margot."

This time Lupita didn't deny the possibility. "She was not at breakfast."

"I know. Helena checked on her and said she was in the shower. We'd better see."

I couldn't shake the terrible feeling that we weren't going to find her. I was scared to death she'd pulled off kidnapping Uncle Jeremiah neatly and quickly, with nobody suspecting a thing. I ran to her room, with Lupita close behind me. I knocked on her door only once before opening it.

From all appearances it would seem that she was *still* in the shower. Behind the closed bathroom door, there was the sound of water hitting the shower stall. I knocked on the door. No answer. I pushed the door open. There was no outline of a human body behind the glass shower door. Sick at heart, I yanked it open and turned off the faucets. The hot-water heater long ago had run out of hot water—only cold remained.

"Why?" Lupita gasped. "Why would she do such a thing?" It was a question she didn't expect an answer to, just one that needed to be expressed. Her face was gray, dazed with disbelief and shock.

I touched her arm gently. "We've got to get help."

The feel of my hand seemed to bring her back into the present. Suddenly she was a bundle of efficient energy. "I'll ring the triangle," she said. "That will gather everybody. Then we can split up and search. We will look everywhere until we find Señor Sloane."

I nodded.

Lupita left. I went back to search Uncle Jeremiah's room, looking for some clue. From what I could tell, Margot hadn't even allowed him to dress. So she couldn't be planning to drive him a long distance, I thought. People might be suspicious of a woman driving an old man dressed in pajamas. Where would she take him? She'd had a three-hour start. I went outside. Never had the desert seemed so big, so isolated. Thinking of Margot, I thought of yesterday. Of Vilagos.

Suddenly, with the clearness of a clairvoyant, I knew that was where they had to be. A car could make it up the other side, Donovan had said. She wouldn't have to dress Uncle Jeremiah to take him there. Ghost towns didn't care what the occupants wore. There was a mine shaft too. I couldn't let my mind dwell on the possibilities that presented, but I had a vivid picture of Margot heaving Uncle Jeremiah into the shaft. If I could just get there fast enough, catch her by surprise before anything happened. . . . I thought about Donovan. I wanted him with me, but it would take time to find him—time Uncle Jeremiah might not have.

An idea was forming. There was the ATV—unless Rudy had taken it. No, he couldn't have, because I had the key in my room. I ran back to my room, took the two keys from the top of the desk, grabbed the helmet out of the closet. I took two seconds to scribble a note to Donovan: *Gone to Vilagos. I think Margot's there.*

The bright-red ATV was still chained to the tree. I wrestled with the lock, threw the chain on the ground, and put the other key in the ignition. From somewhere nearby I could hear Lupita clanging away on the breakfast triangle.

When you're totally focused on something, it's amazing what you can do. It took me only a few seconds and one false start before I was riding out of the ranch toward Silver Dome.

CHAPTER ELEVEN

I followed the same horse trail we'd taken up Silver Dome the morning of the breakfast ride. At least, I hoped it was the same. My sense of direction felt wobbly; every dissecting path sent a tremble of uncertainty in time to the vibrations of the ATV. I stuck to the widest, most-used-looking trail. As long as I was headed in the direction of Silver Dome, I figured I'd hit Vilagos eventually.

I'd hoped I could beat Margot to Vilagos, to surprise her. Exactly how, I had no idea. My mind ran to the idea of tackling her. I should be in better physical condition than she. However, I also knew that someone mentally unbalanced, when faced with opposition, could connect with incredible strength.

And, of course, my primary concern had to be protecting Uncle Jeremiah. Just the stress of discovering someone he cared about was trying to kill him, could. . . . Or if she succeeded in giving him a breathing depressant. . . . What if she'd already killed him? I inhaled some dust and choked, coughing and sneezing.

As I climbed the foothills, the ATV sputtered and lurched. Ahead of me the trail uncoiled like a white snake. I stopped letting myself look ahead too much for fear I'd panic. The path felt booby-trapped. Every stone and fissure caused the ATV to sway and lurch. I had to keep ducking and shifting to avoid low-hanging branches and cacti. Since I knew how easily ATVs could tip over, I had to be careful not to accelerate too quickly and to keep my weight balanced while doing all these maneuvers.

I was sweating; the sun was fiercely hot. I licked my lips. It didn't help. *Water.* I hadn't brought water with me, and I had no idea how long I'd be gone or what I'd run into. How could I have forgotten the basic rule of the desert? I glanced back over my shoulder. Behind me the white roofs of the ranch nestled into the folds of the lumpy hills like a toy village. I couldn't turn back. It would waste too much time. I swerved to avoid a cactus, and a tree branch whacked my helmet so hard it reverberated.

A fork in the trail ahead of me caused me to brake. An orange ribbon dangled from a bare branch of a thorny-looking bush; the other trail was unmarked. The orange was for the bikers, I remembered Rudy saying. The unmarked trail had been stomped flat by horses' hooves. It had to have been the way we went yesterday. Swinging the machine to the right, I followed it. Almost immediately the trail narrowed.

Maybe I'd made a mistake. Maybe I should have followed the marked trail. And already, just knowing I had nothing to quench my thirst, I was feeling so thirsty I could hardly stand it. My throat felt raw; it was hard to swallow.

One of the giant wheels hit a rock at a strange angle and tipped unsteadily to one side. The ATV jolted off the trail, and suddenly I was in loose, sandy dirt. Losing traction briefly, the ATV seemed to be slipping backward. Then it jumped forward and everything was all right.

I had to be getting close. If Margot were already here, I didn't want her to hear the ATV and be warned, and I wasn't sure how much of an incline the ATV could handle. The trail was continually getting steeper. I pulled into a clearing and stopped. I'd go the rest of the way by foot. As I started to take off the helmet, I stopped and left it on, deciding that it would protect me from the sun or, if I slipped, keep me from bashing my brains. Or I could use it to butt Margot, I thought, pushing relentlessly up the hill on foot.

What if I was doing this for nothing? What if she was on the highway, headed for Tucson? She could dispose of Uncle Jeremiah anywhere on a thousand dirt roads. Maybe the idea that she'd choose this place— A family of quail scampered out from under a bush. I nearly screamed. Panting, my heart rattling away a thousand miles a minute, I bent over and tried to catch my breath and calm myself. *Just quail*, I reminded myself. *Nothing scary.*

Looking down, I could no longer see the ranch. Only miles and miles of look-alike country with nothing to distinguish any one part from any other. It looked as if soon I should be able to touch the cloudless, flat, brilliant blue sky. Halfway on its upward climb, the sun was a white-hot blinding circle.

I faced the trail again, all my senses alert for sounds, for wildlife. I had to be getting close, unless I'd totally lost my sense of direction. My shirt was stuck to my body. My sneakers slipped on some loose rocks; I grabbed at a larger rock and steadied myself. The trail turned abruptly to the left, up another steep rise, and suddenly I could see the empty shacks of Vilagos clutched against the sheer cliffs.

Now use your head, I told myself. *You don't want to go marching down Main Street until you look around carefully. And to do that you need to find a safe, sheltered place.* There was a mesquite tree, but it didn't offer as good a view of the place as the rock across a small clearing. If I could make it over to that. . . .

I'm thinking this through calmly and clearly, some detached piece of myself was observing. *Donovan would be proud of me.* It was as if I could see me crouch and dash across the space that felt as big as a football field but probably wasn't. I kept expecting a warning shout, a gunshot. But I made it to the rock and got behind it, breathing heavily. I waited a moment before I looked around it.

She didn't come here, was my first thought. There was no sound. Nothing seemed out of the ordinary. My gaze went from building to building. The old saloon, the two rickety houses, the two-story hotel, the livery stable. Everything was untouched, silent. A couple of birds sat on the handle of a broken-off pump. I saw the ledge where Donovan and I had had breakfast.

Had Margot made it up to the mine? My eyes skimmed the scraped rocks to the mounds that signaled where Donovan had pointed the day before. No, she couldn't have. She couldn't possibly have driven up there. She couldn't have carried Uncle Jeremiah all that way.

Unable to stand the heat of the helmet another second, and afraid that the sun would reflect off it and draw attention to me, I pulled it off my head. My hair was soaking wet and, free of confinement, almost gave the illusion of being cool for a second.

Just as I was about to give up on the idea that Margot had come to Vilagos, I sensed rather than actually saw something flicker on the periphery of my vision. Focusing all my attention, I stared at the hotel, at the blank second-story window facing the street, until my eyes ached from the strain. Then I saw it again. A flash of white.

There's somebody up there. Aware that I'd stopped breathing, I blinked my scratchy eyes and took a shallow, painful breath. Again I saw a quick bob of white. And then there she was—like a ghost peering out the window. It had to be Margot. I pulled back so that she couldn't see me. She was up in the hotel. Undoubtedly Uncle Jeremiah was with her. *What a perfect plot,* I thought, *to condemn Uncle Jeremiah to die alone in a forgotten, forsaken town.* I could see how the irony of this would appeal to her. *From a busy guest ranch to a deserted, rotting hotel.*

All of this over a broken romance? Was that really what had caused her to go over the edge? For some reason Kevin's face appeared in my mind as clearly as if he'd been standing an inch away. I could see his gray eyes, lying eyes as it had turned out. If someone had broken us up in the beginning when a love that felt as much a part of me as breathing. . . . How would I have felt? No matter how I tried to visualize it, I couldn't imagine wanting to hurt or kill anyone. The difference between us lay in the fact that I wouldn't have given up easily. I would have gone after him. . . .

While I was thinking these thoughts, I was stealthily moving, trying to keep hidden by the sparse shadows of the run-down buildings. As long as I stayed close in, Margot wouldn't be as likely to notice me.

I don't know what I heard—a snap, a footstep. I pressed myself back against a rock next to the small, dilapidated house. Margot came out of the hotel, so close to me I could have reached out and touched her. All thoughts of a surprise tackle vanished when I saw that she had a rifle cradled in the crook of her arm. She was wearing sneakers, jeans, and an overly large lilac-colored shirt. Her auburn hair was as wild looking as her frantic glances right and left. She hurried as lightly as a cat off in the opposite direction.

It took me only a second to decide whether to follow her or to go into the hotel to see if Uncle Jeremiah was inside. The boards nailing the door shut had been wrenched off. The door hung open. Inside, many of the floorboards had rotted away, and those that were left were covered with a thick film of dust. There was dust everywhere, mounds almost two inches deep on the windowsills and countertop.

A faint cough filtered down from upstairs.

Watching my step, avoiding places that looked as if they could cave in under pressure, I hurried up, following the sound that came from a room in the front.

I suppose once upon a time this had been the best room in the house. The walls still bore traces of a silky yellow wall covering. There was a rickety chair, but other than that the room had been stripped. Uncle Jeremiah lay in the center, where Margot had dropped him in a heap—like a bag of bones—his bad leg jutting straight out, while his body was curled up.

"Are you all right?" I dropped to my knees, touching his face.

"Judith, you must get away. She's crazy. I think she's going to kill me. Go, please! Save yourself!"

"I'm not going anywhere without you." I stood up. "Let's hope she's taken off." Staying back as far as I could, I looked out the window. There was Matilda about five hundred yards away. Margot was scrounging around in the backseat. As I watched she straightened up, pulling something out. The sound of the door slamming shut carried up in the stillness of the place.

"No such luck. She's coming," I said. "I'm going to hide so I can catch her off guard. I'll get us out of this, and even if I can't, Donovan, Helena, and the others, will be coming soon. They'll help us." Even as I said the words, I wished I'd let them know where I'd gone. There was the note in my room, but it could be overlooked.

"Go, *go!*" Uncle Jeremiah gasped. He coughed, his face turning purple.

I hesitated a second, wishing I could pull him with me or at least help him get into a more comfortable position. But there wasn't time. I headed through a door that was hanging by a thread. It was another, smaller room with absolutely nowhere to hide, I realized with a jarring panic. Margot's footsteps were on the stairs. The only way out of this room was the hallway, and she'd see me. I flattened myself against the wall, trying to breathe shallowly and quietly. If she happened to look into this room as she passed. . . .

But, intent on whatever she was doing, she didn't turn her head. As I was wondering if I could move over so I could see through the door into the room where Uncle Jeremiah was, I nearly let out a gasp. Two inches away from me the boards were completely missing. I could see into the next room as clearly as if I had my own private window. Another step and I would have been standing directly in Margot's line of vision.

What she'd gone to get was a plastic container of water. I stared at it, my throat and stomach clenching and unclenching with such a longing, I could hardly stand it. She dropped the container on the floor across the room from Uncle Jeremiah.

Why would she take him here and then provide him with water? It didn't make sense.

With the back of her hand Margot rubbed at wisps of hair that had fallen over her eyes. "Are you thirsty?" she asked in a pleasant, conversational voice.

If I rushed her, maybe I could catch her off guard. She'd put the gun on the floor, but it was within easy reach, and I'd noticed that her reactions were quick—quicker than my reflexes, I was afraid.

"A little," Uncle Jeremiah answered her.

"I imagine you'll get even thirstier as the day goes on," Margot told him. "It's too bad you wouldn't take the pills. Then you wouldn't have known any of this. You'd have woken up and found yourself here, alone, afraid, hurting. With no one to hear your screams. And the water would be right here, just out of reach."

"Why? Why are you doing this?"

"I want you to suffer—the way you made me suffer." Her voice rose, edged with a terrifying fury. Agitated, she began to pace.

Just get far enough away from the gun, I thought, forcing my gaze away from the water jug and making myself concentrate on the gun.

"I made you suffer? How?"

Good. Keep her talking. I glanced around, looking for a board, anything I could use as a weapon.

"As if you didn't know. When you fired Dan, of course."

"Dan?" Uncle Jeremiah's voice was muffled, confused. He was trying once again to raise himself to a sitting position. His cheek, where it had been resting on the floor, was covered with dust. I blinked, startled by an obvious realization of how careless I'd been. If she looked closely, Margot would see my footprints. The dust had captured them. My tracks led straight to my hiding place.

"Oh, you mean Dan Burr, the wrangler," Uncle Jeremiah said.

"Yes, the wrangler." Margot spit out the words. "Except he was more than just a wrangler to me. He was the man who loved me. We were going to have a life together. Then you fired him. You ruined everything." Her voice as she spoke underwent a change, becoming childlike and thick with unshed tears.

"Margot, I was enforcing my rules. He knew he shouldn't get involved with a guest." His voice was calm, patient, as if he were dealing with a little girl.

The effort that must have taken, considering his position, the pain he was in, his shortness of breath, was unbelievable.

"You were only fifteen. He . . . he was much older. I couldn't let him take advantage—" Uncle Jeremiah coughed.

"He loved me! He was the only person who *ever* loved me." Her voice rose. "I woke up and he was gone. How could you do that to me? I didn't get to say good-bye, give him my address. I didn't even know his last name—" Her voice cracked. "I looked and looked, and I couldn't find his name or where he'd gone. I was all alone again. If only I could have found out where he'd gone. . . ." Her face crumpled.

"So it was you who tried to burn the place down."

"Yes." She wiped at her eyes with the back of her hand. "I hated you. I hated you so much." She was crying harder now. "I still hate you!"

I tried to prepare myself to spring, to knock her down. My breathing felt thick, uneven. I'd been standing so still I'd become rigid. When I moved I'd be apt to be unsteady. I couldn't misjudge; there'd be only one chance.

"Then when the baby came . . . my parents made me give him up too. So I ended up with nobody to love. That's when I knew *you* had to die. You'd taken away everything. So you had to die. Only, no matter what I did, you didn't die. Well, this time you're going to!"

Uncle Jeremiah tried to speak and couldn't catch his breath enough to. He coughed and coughed, his whole body shaking with the effort.

"Margot, I can see I did a terrible thing," Uncle Jeremiah said finally in a voice as soft as a whisper.

He coughed again. "I'm very sorry. I hurt you without meaning to."

"Do you mean that?" The agony etched on Margot's face was very moving in spite of my own fear, the heat, and my incredible thirst. My pain seemed very small compared to the pain I saw reflected in her eyes.

"I just acted—acted like a stubborn fool on a principle, without thinking of the people involved—especially not thinking of a young girl's heart."

Margot took in a gasping breath; several silent sobs rolled through her narrow shoulders.

"And I'm sorry. If I could go back and erase time, I would—"

Uncle Jeremiah's voice broke off into a spasm of coughing. He choked and coughed and choked again. His color turned a bluish gray. He rolled to his side and pressed his hands against his chest, sucking in the dry air.

A look of concern passed over Margot's face, as if she'd snapped back and realized he meant what he said.

Good move, I thought. *You're going to talk her down.*

"What can I do to make it up to you?" he asked softly.

"It's too late."

"Some things are, and I'm sorry. But maybe there's something I can do now. If you'll just let me help—"

"Hey, Judy!" Rudy's voice came floating up like a disembodied spirit. It was such a surprise, it was hard to believe I'd really heard it.

Margot wiped at her face with her shirtsleeve. In a

swift movement she underwent almost a complete transformation. The sad little girl was gone, replaced by a nail-hard, jumpy woman. She grabbed the rifle from the floor with the authority of someone who knew how to use it and who would.

I felt an irrational flash of anger at Rudy's interference. Uncle Jeremiah had been so close to getting her to relax. I could have rushed her. . . .

"If you make any noise, I'll kill him," Margot hissed to Uncle Jeremiah. On tiptoe she darted to the window and glanced out before moving back out of sight. She bit her lower lip, indecision clouding her features.

What was Rudy doing here? I couldn't make my brain click into action and come up with any sensible answer.

"Judy? Are you there?" Rudy's voice drifted up again, closer this time.

Margot shifted the gun, raised it and faced the door. If I heard his footsteps on the stairs, I'd have to yell, warn him. Maybe then I could rush her. My heart was beating so loudly, I could hardly hear, hardly breathe. *Go away!* I silently begged Rudy. *Go away and get help!*

It was as if all three of us were holding our breath. From downstairs came the squeak of the door opening, the sound of Rudy's boots thumping around downstairs. "Judy, where are you?" he called.

How was Uncle Jeremiah managing not to cough, I wondered. I could see from his bulging eyes, his contorted face that he needed to. My legs were numb from standing so stiffly. My toes cramped in my shoes. *Go away, Rudy. Please, go away.*

"Judy!" Rudy's voice came from outside again. Gradually my name got farther away.

Uncle Jeremiah went into a spasm of coughing, burying his face in his arms to muffle the sound. *He doesn't want Rudy hurt,* I thought. Once again I was amazed at his bravery, his determination that nobody beside himself was going to be involved in this life-and-death matter. I concentrated on my own breathing and shifted my weight to ease my legs.

Now that Rudy was gone, I began to worry about making the wrong judgment call. Maybe I should have called out. Knowing there were two of us might have rattled Margot enough. . . . No, she might have just simply shot Uncle Jeremiah. I'd done the right thing.

"Why is he calling for Judith?" Margot demanded. She stared at Uncle Jeremiah suspiciously. Slowly she turned. I could actually see the exact moment that she noticed my footprints. I turned sideways, away from the hole, once again holding my breath, wishing I could make myself invisible.

"You drove her car," Uncle Jeremiah choked out between coughing fits. "He saw the car. That's all."

"Nice try." I could hear the boards creak as Margot moved toward my room. "Judith, I know you're there. Walk out where I can see you. With your hands up."

CHAPTER TWELVE

I moved into the doorway, hands in the air. "Margot," I said, in a desperate attempt to connect with some normal reaction inside her, "Uncle Jeremiah's suffering. He needs help."

"Shut up." She jerked the gun at me, waist high, and motioned with her head for me to go over to Uncle Jeremiah. "Sit down, and keep your hands on your legs where I can see them."

"Last night we were having a good time playing bingo. Today you're holding a gun on me. Somehow I can't get my mind around that."

"Be quiet! I don't want you to talk. I need to think. I can't think if you talk. Especially if you talk nonsense. Why did you come? I mean, how did you know I was here? What am I going to do with you?" The last question came out more like a wail.

"Rudy's here too," I reminded her. "And Helena and Donovan and the others will be along soon—if they aren't here already."

A look of utter confusion passed over her face. "It

171

isn't supposed to go like this. I don't want them here. I don't want to hurt anyone but *him."*

Keep her talking, I thought. "What about the day you took a shot at me? You wanted to hurt me then, didn't you?"

"No. I wanted you to be scared, to go home."

"And when that didn't work, you put the squashed cottontail—"

"Yes. That poor bunny," she said, her voice softening. "I found him on the road." Her eyes darted to Uncle Jeremiah; she nudged his ribs with the tip of the rifle. "Did you mean that at dinner? Did you really pick up the rabbits so I wouldn't see them?"

"Yes."

She blinked as if trying to understand how she could be trying to kill someone who had done that for her.

"You see, he does care about you," I said. My throat had gotten so dry that each word felt as if it tore. "You heard him say he was sorry, that he didn't mean to hurt you."

From somewhere a horse whinnied. There was Rudy's voice again. Donovan's. The words were impossible to make out. I felt hot, feverish, and so thirsty my mind was buzzing with distorted thoughts and images. I had to keep reminding myself what the priorities had to be: Uncle Jeremiah, me; water came last.

"Margot? Margot dear, are you in there? It's Helena."

Margot glanced from me to the window and back to me, her eyes wild. "Go to the window. Tell Helena to leave. Tell her I'll kill you."

"I can't. My throat is too dry." It wasn't hard to push my voice into a raspy whisper. "I need some water first."

"Margot!" It was eerie the way Helena's voice seemed to bounce in and out of all the empty buildings before entering our window.

Margot's finger clicked the trigger. "All right. But hurry. Make her go away."

I got to my feet and walked deliberately, slowly to the water. I couldn't afford any mistakes. Everything counted on my ruse working. Except that it was so hard to concentrate. I had to keep blinking my dry eyes, taking quick breaths. I pried the lid off the container. The fresh scent of water curled up, tempting me. *One little sip*, I thought. *Just one. . . .*

"*Margot!*" This time Helena's voice was louder— as if she were in a concert, standing downstage, projecting her voice as far as she could. It had a remarkable, unnerving effect. I couldn't have directed a more effective scene. Margot flipped her gaze toward the window. Without taking a drink, putting both hands on the bottle, I swung it as hard as I could, the way I used to pitch softball, and let go. It hit Margot squarely in the stomach. I heard the outrush of air. Water splashed everywhere. Margot bent over, clutching her stomach. The rifle dangled, then clattered to the floor.

I sprang, my hands grabbing her wet shirt, pushing her backward. The force of my body knocked her to the floor. As we fell I kicked the rifle out of reach. Margot squirmed and fought. Her fingers clawed at my face, trying to reach my eyes. I straddled her and got her arms above her head. I pressed my knees against her shoulders, keeping them on the floor, and then I just held on for dear life.

There were voices, shouts, footsteps. Beneath me, Margot suddenly stopped struggling and began to cry, a pitiful, high-pitched keening.

Donovan, Rudy, and Helena burst into the room. I was dimly aware that Donovan was beside me, was loosening my hands from Margot's arms. He lifted me away from her. "Rudy!" he shouted.

"I'm right here. I have Margot," Rudy answered. "It's okay."

"Judith, are you all right?" Not waiting for me to speak, Donovan looked me up and down, even turned me around. Relief flooded his face. "You must be. I don't see any blood. You don't seem hurt."

"I'm fine," I assured him. "It's Uncle Jeremiah. . . ."

"He's all right," Helena called out. "I'm tending to him. I've brought his inhalant and water." She was on the floor beside him, supporting his head so that he could drink from the canteen she held.

"You took an awful chance," Donovan was saying. "Why didn't you come to the stable and get me?"

"As usual, I didn't think. I wanted to get here first and surprise her, which I did—almost." Uncle Jeremiah was still taking sips of water. I could wait before I asked for some.

There was the sound of a scuffle as Margot tried to shake free of Rudy's grip. "That's it," he said. "I'm going to make sure you don't cause any more trouble." Rudy yanked his belt free from his jeans, looping it over Margot's wrists.

"No," she shrieked. "Let go of me!"

"Don't tie her," Uncle Jeremiah said, craning his neck around the crook of Helena's arm. "She needs help, not more punishment."

"Jerry," Rudy argued, "she's dangerous."

"I agree," Donovan said.

"No. Uncle Jeremiah's right," I said. "Can't you just hold on to her?"

"Okay." Rudy didn't look convinced, but he dropped the belt and simply held both her wrists with one of his large hands. Like magic, Margot's shoulders slumped and she stopped struggling.

"If you've had enough water, Uncle Jeremiah, I'd like some," I said.

Helena tossed me the canteen. I unscrewed the top and took a long, slow swallow. It was wonderful, the best-tasting drink I'd ever had. I took another swallow and another, then screwed the top back on the canteen.

"I don't understand where Max is," Rudy said.

"Max is here?" I asked.

"Near here. We were checking out the trails, retying the ribbons— Hey, wait a minute. I'll bet it was *Margot* who changed the ribbons. It *was* you, wasn't it?"

Margot shot him a contemptuous look and refused to answer.

"It doesn't matter, Rudy," Helena interjected. "What's done is done."

I slid a sideways glance at Donovan, who was talking to Rudy about the logistics of getting back to the ranch. There was the car, two horses, two ATVs, and too many people. . . . The conversation faded out as I concentrated on the fineness of his profile, the way his hair curled around his ears, and how his glasses defined the bridge of his nose. He meant so much to me. How could I go back to Chicago and leave him?

"Could I have the water?" Margot's voice broke through my thoughts. "Please," she added.

I handed the canteen to Rudy. He jiggled it, trying to loosen the top while he still held on to Margot.

"I'm sorry. I didn't think," I said. "Here, let me. . . ."

"I've got it."

With a sudden quick movement Margot wrenched free. Rudy shouted, grabbed for her, and got the tail end of her shirt, which, as she lunged forward, ripped off in his hand.

Before any of us could react, she was at the window. With amazing agility she sprang up onto the ledge—and jumped. There was a terrible cracking, the sound of wood ripping, a dull thud—and then absolute silence.

"Oh, no!" Somehow my feet carried me to the window. Margot lay in a crumpled heap, not moving.

Rudy reacted first. He ran from the room and down the stairs. Donovan had come up beside me; I could feel the pressure of his hand on my shoulder.

"I should go," I said.

"Stay here. There's nothing you can do," Donovan answered.

I could hear Helena murmuring to Uncle Jeremiah. It was as if time had stopped, as if we were all caught in a suspended moment, hearts ticking like clocks waiting for a bomb to go off. Waiting for Rudy to tell us what we were all fearing.

Rudy reached Margot quickly. We could see him trying to rouse her without success. He put his head against her chest, listening for her heartbeat. Finally he looked up at us and shook his head.

My throat caught. I swallowed. "She's dead," I said.

No one spoke. We were too dazed. I had a fleeting moment of wondering if I were to blame somehow. If I should have insisted that Rudy tie her. I shook the thought away. No, we'd done what we thought was the most humane thing. It hadn't worked; that was all.

Rudy stopped in the doorway without coming in, both hands on the doorframe as if it were the only thing holding him up. "She's dead," he repeated. "She hit the railing over the balcony, fell through the old sign. It looks like her neck is broken."

"I wanted to help her," Uncle Jeremiah said weakly.

We all hastened to assure him that we knew that.

"Margot painted herself into a corner," Helena said. "No one here is to blame for what happened. We did the best we could."

She was right; I think we all felt that. Still, a sadness filled the hot room, and no one spoke for a few minutes, each of us needing time to accept what had just happened.

"I think we ought to go back," Donovan said finally. "That is, if you feel well enough, Jeremiah."

Uncle Jeremiah said he did. Donovan and Rudy decided that Donovan would drive Uncle Jeremiah back to the ranch and send Raymond up with the truck for Margot's body. Helena said she'd wait with Rudy and drive the truck back so that the wrangler could ride one horse and lead the other. Somehow Rudy and Max would get the ATVs back to Rudy's place.

The next two hours were a blur of activity and confusion. We sent Raymond back to Vilagos with the truck. We talked to the sheriff. We got Uncle Jeremiah squared away—a bath, clean clothes, and more liquid to fight dehydration.

As the guests trickled back in, we told them what had happened. All of them, except for Dr. Morgansting, had been helping in the search. Dr. Morgansting, according to an outraged Sophie, had packed up his luggage and demanded that a ride to Tucson be arranged for him. If he'd wanted this kind of violence, he could have stayed at home and left his front door unlocked or gone for a walk after dark, he'd told her.

The next task was calling Margot's parents. Uncle Jeremiah insisted that this was his responsibility. We could come with him, but he would do the actual phoning. Donovan wheeled him over to the office. While he dialed, the two of us leaned against the counter and stared out at the clipped patch of grass.

From what we could overhear, it sounded as if Margot's parents had been trying for years to make peace with her. Like Uncle Jeremiah, they regretted what had happened. But Margot had been too mentally ill to accept anything they had to offer. They wanted Margot's body sent back East for burial. As Uncle Jeremiah's voice droned on, making the arrangements, my mind drifted. Margot's sad story had been resolved in a way.

I tried to find the right words to express how I was

feeling to Donovan. It turned out he'd been thinking more or less the same thing.

"What about 'our' story?" Donovan asked suddenly.

"Our story?" Not wanting to interrupt Uncle Jeremiah's conversation, we'd been whispering, which gave a nice, intimate feel to what we were saying.

"What kind of an ending is it going to have?" He wove his fingers through mine and lifted our hands so that he could kiss my fingers where they wrapped around his. "Are you really going to go back to Chicago to some hospital? Or—"

"What he's asking is if you're going to stay here, help your old uncle, and keep the place afloat," Uncle Jeremiah interrupted. He wheeled himself around the counter between us and the door. "No one's leaving until I get the answer I want. I want you both to stay here. We'll convert the Silver Sands Ranch into the Silver Sands Camp for disabled children."

"I don't see how your idea would work," I said. "You need a lot of equipment to do physical therapy —it would cost money. A lot of money."

"Money, what's money? If you'll just say yes, I'll make all the financial arrangements," Uncle Jeremiah said. "I wasn't selling Silver Sands because of a lack of money, you know." Two bright pink spots of color had come into his cheeks. In spite of this morning's ordeal he looked almost chipper.

"It's tempting," I said. "But I need to think—"

There was the sound of tires crunching on gravel. We could see the truck pull in, hear urgent shouts.

We hurried out. Raymond was driving. Rudy and

Helena were in the back, hovering over another person.

Donovan and I flashed each other a "what now?" look.

"It's Max, Judy!" Rudy shouted as soon as he saw me. "He's hurt bad."

I scrambled into the truck bed. Max seemed to be unconscious. There was an ugly cut over his left eye. Rudy had tried to staunch the blood with his shirt. I heard myself telling Helena how to press her fingers just in front of Max's left ear to stop the blood flow from the deep wound.

As I checked Max over, I was dimly aware that Lupita, Oscar, and several guests were peering over the side, their faces taut with concern.

"The ATV tipped over on him," Rudy explained.

I could feel that Max's collarbone was broken and possibly his shoulder. "He's got to be taken to a hospital. He may have internal injuries," I said. I asked Donovan to get several blankets and roll them to act as supports so that Max would be as comfortable as possible on the drive.

When Donovan returned I took the blankets and pushed them around Max's inert form. I offered to go with them, but Rudy and Lupita said they could manage. Lupita took Helena's place. The bleeding seemed to have stopped, but I made sure Lupita knew what to do if it started again. She assured me that if the small community hospital thirty miles away couldn't provide the care Max needed, they could get transportation to a hospital in Tucson for him.

As soon as the truck pulled away, Donovan and

Oscar left in the station wagon to bring back Margot's body.

"Is there anything you don't know how to handle?" Donovan asked me two hours later. We were foraging around the kitchen, putting out cold cuts, cheese, and bread for the guests to make their own sandwiches. I'd had a shower and changed into shorts and a halter top and was temporarily cool. The fan whirled overhead, stirring the air. Lupita had called to say that Max was resting comfortably in the hospital—that he had made the trip there without any further complications.

"Actually, there's a lot. My job has taught me how to deal with emergencies. It's deciding what I want to do when I have time to think that's hard for me." I put down the ladle I was using to empty a mustard jar, which was large enough to feed a family of giants, into a bowl. "I've been thinking a lot about Uncle Jeremiah's idea."

Donovan stopped slicing a loaf of French bread and looked at me. "And?"

"I'd like to give it a try."

The fan purred away; somewhere a clock was ticking. A part of me was recording this as I watched a look of pure joy spread over Donovan's face. He let out a whoop and swooped me up in the air so suddenly that one of my shoes fell off. "I was hoping," he said, pressing his face against my hair. "You'll never know how much I was hoping you'd say that."

"It goes against every sensible bone in my body," I said. "Mom will probably have a fit, but I don't care. All I know is that I don't want to leave you. And just maybe, with enough planning, we can make this camp idea work."

To my amazement Mom didn't have a fit. She was all for it. Even Rudy, when we told him our plans as we visited Max in the hospital, thought it was a good idea. I'd half expected him to be depressed about the outcome of things. But he'd gone back to being the nothing-daunts-me Rudy I'd first met. He and Max were full of plans about setting up another recreational area near Yuma.

Once Uncle Jeremiah, Donovan, and I sat down and began brainstorming, I became totally caught up in Uncle Jeremiah's and Donovan's excitement. We'd need a therapy pool. And if we tore down the walls between two of the guest rooms in the main lodge, we'd have a room big enough for the exercise equipment. The whole main lodge could be air-conditioned.

Donovan said he'd like to keep the campsite down in the cottonwoods. One of his ideas was to teach the children how to construct a living place outdoors. He also wanted to continue his experiments with solar heating. But he readily agreed that he'd had enough of roughing it, especially now that the weather was getting so hot. He thought it would be nice to climb into clean sheets at night and rely on Lupita's cooking.

On the last night of the guest season, the few guests who were left—Helena and Mr. and Mrs. Jamison—gathered once again in the living room for a farewell concert.

When Helena had finished singing, Donovan and I slipped outside. The air was warm, with a clear, light texture I'd come to associate with being Arizona. The moon was high in the sky. Arm in arm we went far enough away from the lodge that we wouldn't be interrupted and sat down on the lawn. This would be our last evening together for a while. I was taking a flight back to Chicago the following evening, and Donovan was heading back to L.A. in a few days to settle unfinished business there. We planned to meet back here in a month.

"We've talked almost nonstop over the last few days about our plans for the camp," Donovan said. "Tonight I'd like to talk about us."

"That sounds good to me. I know where I stand. I love you," I blurted out in my usual way. "I know it may be too soon and that you may not feel the same way. But I'm prepared to wait."

Donovan cupped my face in his large, calloused hands, running his thumbs along my jawbone, caressing my chin. "Scientists aren't supposed to believe in love at first sight," he said in a semiserious voice.

"Don't worry about that," I teased. "The first time I saw you, you barely noticed me. So I know it wasn't love at first sight for you."

"Later on that same night, when you'd been drugged, you looked so vulnerable . . . that's when I realized I was feeling something unusual toward you. Something that felt protective."

"Kind of what you feel toward those little injured animals you care for?"

"Kind of." He kissed me once, twice, his lips tender and seeking a response from mine.

"Then," he went on, "the next morning when you showed up and insisted I share my trout— Well, you hooked me just as surely as I'd hooked them. From that moment on I was yours."

"Really?" It seemed hard to believe, although, judging by his kisses, it was certainly true now.

"Really. In fact, I've been thinking: If it's all right with you, I might come to Chicago in a few weeks and meet your family. Then maybe you could fly to L.A. and meet Mom. Then in the fall, right before the camp opens, maybe we could be married—here at Silver Sands. What do you think?"

Maybe most people would think everything was happening too soon. But, then, I wasn't like most people; I'd learned that long ago.

And there wasn't even a shadow of a doubt in my mind when I said yes. Yes, it was all right—better than all right. It was just plain wonderful!